HEART OF ICE

Germany, 1938. The escalation of anti-Jewish attacks prompts Kurt's mother to send him to England but when he's boarding the ship, he's mistakenly given a stranger's suitcase. Whilst attempting to return it to its owner, he meets Eleanor but his humble circumstances discourage him from meeting her again. Their paths cross later at RAF Holsmere where Kurt is a pilot and Eleanor a WAAF but is there too much death and destruction to consider taking a chance on love?

DAWN KNOX

HEART OF ICE

Complete and Unabridged

LINFORD
Leicester

First published in Great Britain in 2019

First Linford Edition
published 2020

*A catalogue record for this book is available
from the British Library.*

ISBN 978–1–4448–4623–2

Published by
Ulverscroft Limited
Anstey, Leicestershire

Set by Words & Graphics Ltd.
Anstey, Leicestershire
Printed and bound in Great Britain by
TJ Books Limited, Padstow, Cornwall

This book is printed on acid-free paper

was established in 1972 to provide funds for research, diagnosis and treatment of eye diseases. Examples of major projects funded by the Ulverscroft Foundation are:-

- The Children's Eye Unit at Moorfields Eye Hospital, London
- The Ulverscroft Children's Eye Unit at Great Ormond Street Hospital for Sick Children
- Funding research into eye diseases and treatment at the Department of Ophthalmology, University of Leicester
- The Ulverscroft Vision Research Group, Institute of Child Health
- Twin operating theatres at the Western Ophthalmic Hospital, London
- The Chair of Ophthalmology at the Royal Australian College of Ophthalmologists

You can help further the work of the Foundation by making a donation or leaving a legacy. Every contribution is gratefully received. If you would like to help support the Foundation or require further information, please contact:

1

January, 1939

'Karl Rosenberg!' the sandy-haired man yelled, his hands cupped around his mouth to help his voice carry over the uproar.

'What did he say? What's that ticket collector shouting?' The girl gripped Kurt's arm tightly. Her eyes were round, damp and overly bright.

'I can't hear,' said Kurt, gently removing her hand from his arm and easing his way through the crowd, closer to the sandy-haired official.

'Karl Rosenberg!' the man bellowed again but his voice was half-drowned by a young boy's screams and by the chatter of the queues of children lining up in the warehouse-like departure hall, about to board the ferry to England.

The official shouted again, and this time, Kurt was sure he heard him say

Rosenberg — which was his surname.

No one was owning up to being Karl Rosenberg and the more the man shouted, the more his eyebrows drew together in annoyance.

Kurt hesitated.

'Didn't you say your name was Rosenberg?' The girl who'd grabbed his arm earlier, had wriggled through the throng and joined him again.

'Yes, but my name's Kurt, not Karl.'

'Perhaps you'd better ask. You never know.'

The girl's eyes filled with tears. She'd spent most of the journey from Berlin to the Hook of Holland crying for the parents she'd left behind.

Kurt stepped forward. 'I'm Kurt Rosenberg,' he said, holding out his papers towards the man. 'Do you want me?'

'Kurt?' The official hesitated and glanced back at the ticket collector at the head of the next queue. He frowned, inspected Kurt's papers, then shrugged. 'Well, you should be ashamed of yourself worrying your sisters like that!' he said.

'I . . . I'm . . .'

'Move along now!' said the official.

'What did he want?' the girl asked when Kurt stepped back into the queue.

'No idea. He told me not to worry my sisters.'

'I thought you were travelling on your own.'

'I am.'

'So where are your sisters?'

'Back home in Berlin with Mutti.'

'Tickets, please!' the man at the door shouted, allowing the girl to go through the barrier.

He looked at Kurt's papers.

'Rosenberg?' he said, barring Kurt's way with his arm. 'Just wait here a moment, son.'

The girl looked back in alarm but was ushered out to the dock area, lost from Kurt's sight.

'Don't look so worried, the ferry won't leave without you!' the ticket inspector added with a smile. 'There's a fearsome storm out there. You'll be glad I kept you back.' He winked.

The sandy-haired man who'd spoken to Kurt earlier appeared carrying a small, brown leather suitcase which he handed to Kurt.

'Now, for goodness sake, keep your wits about you. As soon as you find your sisters, stay with them. And don't lose your luggage.' He clicked his tongue and strode off.

'But this isn't mine,' Kurt said.

'Right, move along now,' said the ticket inspector, ushering him towards the door and turning to the next child in the queue.

Sleet blew almost horizontally across the dock and small figures clutching bags and cases were being urged by officials to hurry towards the gang-planks and up onto the enormous ship.

Kurt fought against the biting wind, holding his own suitcase and the one he'd just been given. None of the adults shepherding the children on to the ferry looked as though they wanted to deal with queries — presumably they were keen to get the passengers on board and go back inside.

Kurt decided that as soon as he was on the ship, he'd find someone to take the suitcase so it could be reunited with its owner. There'd obviously been a mix-up and he felt responsible for having stepped forward when the sandy-haired man had asked for Karl Rosenberg.

Once on board the ferry, Kurt made his way into the salon. It was packed. All the seats were taken, and many children were sitting on the floor, surrounded by luggage. Kurt picked his way to a space in a corner. Each time the door opened, a vicious blast of icy wind blew in, which was probably why the corner wasn't already occupied.

Kurt was reluctant to leave the spot despite the draughts. Knowing the crossing from the Hook of Holland to Harwich would take most of the night, he wanted something to lean against. So he sat with the stranger's case on his lap, on top of his own.

He'd tried to hand it to one of the crew members who'd come into the salon to warn people to stay where they were and not to go on deck. Once they left the harbour, there would be rough seas and the deck was slippery. But the man said he was too busy to do anything about lost property; it would be best to hand it in as Kurt left the ship.

The sailor had been correct; there was a tremendous swell as they left the relative calm of the harbour. It was impossible to walk without staggering drunkenly. As the ferry pitched and rolled, many passengers' faces were white with fear, others with green with seasickness.

Despite the lurching motion, most of the children fell asleep, their limp bodies swaying as the ship fought the mountainous waves. For many, it was their first time away from home without the parents and siblings they'd been torn from earlier that morning. They were emotionally drained.

Kurt folded up his scarf and laid it like a cushion on his cases, then crossing his arms over it, he rested his head on them and tried to sleep.

He'd had a shock when the man had told him off for worrying his sisters. For a second, his heart had been full of hope, thinking that Inge and Renate had somehow been able to join him. But that simply wasn't possible.

His sisters were in their early twenties, too old to be allowed a place on the Kindertransport train. Anyway, neither of them would have left Mutti. Kurt hadn't wanted to leave her either, but she'd insisted. He'd rather have stayed with his family and faced whatever the Nazis had in store for the Jews.

At only sixteen, Kurt was the man of the family since his father was arrested the previous year.

Professor Rosenberg had been dragged from his lecture hall at the Friedrich-Wilhelms-Universität, in front of his students, after being accused of not only being Jewish, but also of speaking out publicly against the Nazi regime. The university authorities had telephoned Kurt's mother and when she'd made enquiries at the police station, she'd been told her husband had been taken to a concentration camp for 're-education'.

A few days later, Frau Rosenberg lost her position as an English teacher in a local high school because the headmaster considered it undesirable that his pupils should be taught by a Jew. Inge and Renate were also dismissed from their teaching posts and finally, it was decided that Kurt would no longer attend school.

He was very relieved because the teacher had been victimising him for some time. On several occasions Kurt had been made to stand on a chair in front of the class while Herr Bernstein had humiliated him by pointing out to the other pupils why Jews were little better than animals and that it was unfair they should have to share a class with him. Some of his classmates had begun to turn on Kurt, having been encouraged by their teacher's cruelty.

Then in November, 1938, came Kristallnacht — or Crystal Night — when so much glass was smashed, it lay in the streets like crystals.

It began on the evening of Wednesday, the ninth of November. Kurt had already gone to bed. His sisters were playing their violins, accompanying Mutti on the piano in their large apartment. They lived just off Kurfürstendamm, the fashionable boulevard in Berlin, well-known for its leisure and nightlife — and its Jewish businesses.

Several explosions in quick succession caused tremors to be felt in the Rosenbergs' apartment. Kurt came out of his bedroom to find his mother and sisters peeping through the curtains, their faces ashen with shock.

'Shouldn't we go to help?' he asked, assuming there'd been an accident. Mutti had merely turned out the lights and gathered all her children to her.

'What's happening? Why aren't we helping?' Kurt asked.

'Hush, Kurt,' Inge said gently, 'we'd only be targets if we went out.'

They remained in the grand sitting room, listening to the mayhem taking place on the Kurfürstendamm and beyond. Shattering glass, falling masonry and screams filled the night sky which was lit by the dull, red glow of burning buildings.

By first light on Thursday, the chaos had calmed. Yet it was several days before Frau Rosenberg would allow any of them out of the apartment. Despite his mother's reluctance, Kurt insisted someone would need to go out to buy milk and food. He was small for his age and had a young face, so he argued he'd draw less attention than any of the women of his family. Who would bother with a young boy?

He bought milk, bread and a newspaper.

When he returned, he was shaking.

'The synagogue's gone!' he said.

'Gone?'

'Destroyed! There's nothing left! Just a pile of burned beams, bricks and broken glass.'

Mutti had moaned and caught him to her.

'I shouldn't have let you go, Kurt.'

'Someone had to go, Mutti. And that someone should be me . . . until Vater comes home.'

The newspaper brought more harrowing news. It had been bad enough that the Nazi Stormtroopers and Hitler Youth had targeted so many Jewish homes, synagogues and businesses in their beloved city of Berlin but apparently, such attacks had occurred on the same night in many German towns and cities, as well as in Austria and other countries.

It was obvious the action had been organised.

'Let's leave Germany, Mutti! We're not wanted here!' Inge said. 'Let's go to England. You're English and Vater's half-English. Surely they'll look after us until we get back on our feet.'

Slowly Frau Rosenberg shook her head.

'What happens if your father comes home and finds us gone? No, I must wait for him.'

In the end, she'd gone to the Reich Representation of Jews in Germany and arranged for Kurt to go to England, to stay with his father's cousin. Passage was being organised for children under the age of seventeen, so Inge and Renate weren't eligible, but they had already made up their minds they wouldn't leave their mother.

'Well, I don't want to leave you all!' Kurt had protested but his mother pleaded with him and eventually, he'd been persuaded.

Now, thrown this way and that on the floor of the ferry, amid the subdued snuffles and sobs as the ship lurched, Kurt wished he was still at home. Surely nothing could be as bad as the emptiness he now felt inside. One of the crew members had dimmed the lighting so that those who were able, could sleep and Kurt looked around for the girl who'd attached herself to him at the station in Berlin. He realised with dismay he couldn't even remember her name — was it Brigitte? Brunhilde, perhaps? He was sure it had begun with a B.

The girl's mother had begged him to take care of her as the children were propelled forwards to the train, desperate for someone to look out for her little girl travelling on her own to a strange land. He'd agreed, and had done his best but he'd only just managed to calm the girl by the time they reached the German border.

Then the train had stopped and all the children had been ordered out of the carriages. They were lined up on the station platform while the soldiers went through their bags. Kurt had seen several children dragged away into the station office. As far as he knew, they hadn't re-boarded the train.

Brigitte or Brunhilde or whatever her

name was, had been distraught and exhausted herself crying all the way through Holland. He'd done his best to be kind but he, too, was afraid and grief-stricken.

Now he'd lost the girl, through no fault of his own. He felt guilty that he hadn't fulfilled his promise to her mother.

The wind had calmed slightly and Kurt wondered if they would dock soon. His legs and bottom were numb, and his back stiff from bending over resting his head on his hands for hours.

Gradually, it grew lighter and Kurt decided to go on deck and see if land was in sight. Several others joined him, braving the biting wind and the fine, salt spray, to peer towards the misty horizon, searching for the shore of the country which was offering them sanctuary.

Finally, land came into view. Some of the boys pointed excitedly, although most of those who'd joined them on deck were too tired, too anxious and too miserable to do more than gaze silently at the mouth of the harbour which was marked by a green light on one side and red on the other.

Kurt remembered his first sight of England, many years ago when the Rosenberg family had visited Mutti's parents in London. He'd asked why there weren't two red lights or two green and Vater had explained it was how harbour entrances were marked; what guided sailors home. Now the lights were guiding countless children away from their homes.

As they waited for the gangplanks to be ready, Kurt tried again to hand the suitcase to one of the crew members, who said it was probably best to wait until he'd disembarked and then give it to one of the people who'd be escorting them to London.

He tried again with a ginger-haired lady who was clutching a clipboard and ticking off children's names, but it was obvious her mind was on her charges and not on a misplaced suitcase.

'It's probably best if you look inside

and find out if there's an address. You can write and tell the owner you've got it . . . You, there! If I've ticked you off, you have to stay with me! Don't wander off or you'll get left behind!' She rushed over to a small boy who was drifting away from the group of children she'd already collected.

If there was an address inside the case, it would probably be for a place in Germany. Obviously, the owner was fleeing to England, so how would that help Kurt return it?

It seemed no one wanted to take responsibility for the suitcase. He'd have to do as the ginger-haired woman suggested. However, it was too busy in the arrivals hall to open the case and look. He was also afraid he'd be left behind as the woman had impressed on them they must stay with her or they might miss the train to London, so when a lady offered him a cup of tea and a bun, he placed both cases between his feet and accepted them gratefully. It had been many hours since he'd eaten.

Finally, the ginger-haired woman shouted out the names of the children in her group. Once satisfied they had her attention, she led them all towards the station.

'What's she saying?' a plump girl asked. 'I wish I understood what was going on.'

'Stay with me,' Kurt said. 'I speak English.'

'You're so lucky,' the girl said. 'I only know a few words. It's going to be hard enough living in a new country with a new family without having to learn a new language too.'

For the first time, Kurt realised how fortunate he was, not only to be able to speak English perfectly without a German accent but also to be going to stay with his own family. Not that he knew his father's cousin — but it would be better than staying with strangers. Wouldn't it?

* * *

The plump girl stayed with Kurt all the way to Liverpool Street Station although once aboard the train, there had been no more instructions she needed to understand. He knew the trial would begin for her when she was handed over to the family who'd offered to take her in — and Kurt wouldn't be there for that. He felt he'd helped a bit; if he'd let down Brigitte or Brunhilde, yesterday, at least he'd helped Katya today.

Kurt wiped a circle in the condensation on the train window and they looked with dismay at the grimy, run-down buildings of London's East End.

'It's nothing like our beautiful Berlin, is it, Kurt? I know we're not quite a thousand kilometres from home but it seems like it could be millions,' Katya said wistfully.

Kurt discovered she'd lived with her parents further along the Kurfürstendamm. She too came from a wealthy family, her father owning a successful furniture shop.

'All gone now,' she told Kurt with a sob, 'burned to the ground on Kristallnacht.'

'Well, at least we'll be safe here in England,' said Kurt. 'No more looking over your shoulder for members of the Hitler Youth.'

'No, but no more Mutti and Vater either . . . ' Katya said sadly.

She'd asked for Kurt's address so she could write when she got to her new home, but Kurt didn't know where Vater's cousin lived. They merely said goodbye and he waved as she was led away by the ginger-haired woman.

He was suddenly seized by panic. He hadn't expected there to be so many people in the station. If he'd thought about it at all, he'd have imagined Jacob Rosenberg standing there with his wife, Sylvia, and three sons, waving at him and then rushing forward to greet him. But in this crush of people, how was he going to know them?

How were they going to know him?

And what if they didn't come for him?

The ginger-haired lady came to the rescue.

'You wouldn't be . . . um . . . let me see . . . ' she consulted her list, 'Ah, yes! Kurt Rosenberg?'

'Yes!' he said, grateful he wasn't abandoned.

'Mr Rayment's waiting over there for you. He's by the newspaper seller, see?' she said, pointing. Then as soon as she thought his gaze had followed her finger, she was off to shepherd a group of children towards their new families.

Rayment? There was some mistake. Vater's cousin was called Jacob Rosenberg. But perhaps it was a driver, come to pick him up. With a case in either hand, Kurt made his way through the crowds towards the newspaper seller and the skinny, hunched man standing next to him.

Kurt hoped he wasn't the driver. It looked as though he was having problems seeing, as he blinked repeatedly, then took his spectacles off his nose. He polished them on his sleeve and then replacing them, he peered into the crowd.

'Mr Rayment?' Kurt said, reaching the man.

'Ah, Kurt, my boy!' Mr Rayment said and held out his claw-like hand. 'Welcome to London.'

They shook hands.

'Is Jacob Rosenberg coming?' Kurt asked.

'I'm afraid Jacob Rosenberg is no more,' the man said with a smile.

Kurt's mouth fell open in alarm. Where would he stay if his father's cousin couldn't take him in?

Mr Rayment laughed. 'No need to worry. I'll explain everything on our way home.'

'Home?' said Kurt, worried he shouldn't leave with a man he didn't know and hadn't heard of.

Mr Rayment tapped his beak-like nose. 'All will be revealed.' He picked up one of Kurt's suitcases and turned to leave the station concourse.

What choice did Kurt have? If he

didn't follow the stranger, he'd be left in London on his own with nowhere to stay. Grabbing the other case, he dodged after the skinny, hunched Mr Rayment.

Once outside the station, there were too many people to be able to walk side by side. Kurt wondered if they were going to find a cab or perhaps catch a bus but they continued to walk.

Back in Berlin, Mutti had placed some bank notes inside his shoe and Kurt felt them rucking under his foot as he tried to keep up with Mr Rayment. In the other shoe, Mutti had put a gold locket and chain, containing a photo of her and Vater in one side, Renate and Inge in the other.

'To remind you of us,' Mutti had said as she took the necklace from her own neck and tucked it into the toe of his shoe.

Kurt could feel the locket pressing into his toe. The chain had slipped and was now under his sole, chafing and rubbing through his sock.

But at least the money and locket were safe. Had Mutti put them in his luggage, they would've been confiscated by the border guards when the Kindertransport train crossed from Germany into Holland. His valuables, however, had made it safely to England — even if they were aggravating his feet at every step.

'So, young Kurt,' Mr Rayment said when the crowds had thinned and they were walking side by side, 'I must explain. I am your father's cousin.'

'Then why did you say Jacob Rosenberg is no more?'

'Because I no longer use that name. I'm Jack Rayment — a British citizen. My family are British too. While you're staying with me, I'd like you to take the surname Rayment as well. Perhaps change Kurt to . . . umm . . . How d'you feel about Ken? Or Keith?'

'No!' said Kurt, aghast. 'Kurt was the name Mutti and Vater gave me — '

'Mother and Father!' Jack said sharply. 'Don't speak German. I don't want to hear it and neither will anyone else . . . All right, we'll keep the name Kurt. It helps that your mother taught you to speak perfect English and you don't have any trace of a German accent. People won't suspect you're German or Jewish, unless you give them cause.'

Kurt was appalled.

'But I thought it was safe in England! I thought Jews were accepted here!'

'And so they are. But it doesn't do to tempt fate. It doesn't matter where you go in the world, there are always people who hate for hate's sake. The people I live among are, by and large, Cockneys. Big-hearted people, friendly and loyal — once you're one of them. And I aim to be one of them. If you've got any sense, you will too.'

Cockney. That was a word Kurt hadn't heard before. What sort of people were these Cockneys?

They walked on silently and Kurt looked around with dismay. The buildings were old and dilapidated, with rusty railings and paint peeling from doors and window frames. The further they walked, the more decrepit the buildings became. The people who passed them were dressed shabbily, some even in rags, and Kurt was surprised to see a few boys kicking a tin can down the road with bare feet.

Mutti had told him Jacob Rosenberg owned a well-to-do tailor shop in London, where he made suits for the rich and famous. But when Kurt saw the small, dingy shop, over which hung the sign *Rayment Tailors*, he doubted anyone with money would come to this place. The clothes displayed in the window were neither stylish nor elegant.

A bell tinkled as Jack opened the door to the shop. The smell of dust and something Kurt couldn't identify assaulted his nostrils. As they entered, a small, thin woman in a drab, grey dress and shawl rushed out of a room at the back.

Jack introduced his wife, Sylvia, and then three dark-haired ragamuffin boys appeared — their sons, Benjamin, the eldest, at ten years of age, Joseph aged eight and four-year-old Mark.

'Come into the kitchen,' said Sylvia clutching the patched, grey shawl around her gaunt shoulders. Kurt noticed the swelling of her stomach, showing another child was on the way.

'I expect you're hungry after your long journey,' she said. 'Well, sit down at the table and we'll eat. The boys are starving. But aren't boys always starving?'

The table was covered in a clean oilcloth and Kurt could see that although Jack was clearly poor, the house was scrupulously clean. Well — as clean as it could be with all the bundles of rags which were piled up at one end of the room.

Sylvia ladled stew out of a large, black saucepan while the three boys watched, their dark eyes large and round. Benjamin's gaze didn't leave the contents of the bowl he carried to Kurt and the two other boys glowered at him as he picked up his spoon. Glancing around, Kurt noticed all the bowls were half full of thin soup which contained a few lumps of something Kurt couldn't identify.

Were the boys resentful because the food had to be stretched to yet another member of the family? Kurt was horrified to think this might be the case. And worst of all, Sylvia hardly had anything in her bowl.

After the meal, Kurt slipped his shoe off and took out the bank notes Mutti had given him before he'd left.

'This is some pocket money for you, so you can get about in London. Perhaps go to some museums or art galleries,' she'd said — but Kurt knew the life his mother had imagined he'd lead was very different from this . . . Kurt tried to think of the word . . . slum. Yes, that was it — slum.

He wasn't sure if it was good manners or not but nevertheless, he took the money and placed it on the table in front of Jack.

'Mutt . . . Mother gave me this to help pay for my keep. I hope you can change it to sterling.'

Jack's eyes bulged and his hand clamped down on the money as he pocketed it.

'Very kind of her, I'm sure,' said Jack.

'Very kind indeed.' Sylvia had tears in her eyes.

* * *

Kurt's bed was a mattress placed on the floor in the eaves of the attic where the roof sloped so steeply, there wouldn't have been room for a bedstead — assuming one had been available.

He shared with the three boys who slept together in one bed, two lying with their heads to the wall and Mark, the youngest, lying the other way round — like sardines in a can, Kurt thought.

His mattress was lumpy and torn in one corner.

'The rats got it,' Benjamin remarked

when he saw Kurt staring at the stuffing.

But Kurt was too tired to care. Benjamin blew out the candle, and Kurt undressed in the darkness. Taking his mother's heart-shaped locket out of his shoe, he fumbled with the clasp, fastening it around his neck. It was obviously a woman's necklace but it wouldn't be seen under his shirt. And that was where it would stay — to keep it safe and to hold his family close to his own heart. His last thought as he drifted to sleep was that he hadn't opened the stranger's suitcase, but it was too dark now to see anything.

The next morning, when he woke, the three young boys had already gone downstairs. Being alone, Kurt rolled on to his side and, careful not to hit his head on the sloping ceiling, he slid Karl Rosenberg's suitcase towards him, then tried the clasps, hoping they wouldn't be locked.

They weren't. He clicked them open and raised the lid slowly, unsure of looking at someone else's property. But how else could he return it?

There were no markings inside of the lid to indicate a name or address and it looked as if it simply contained clothes. Kurt was disappointed but, he told himself, what else would the suitcase of a Kindertransport boy be likely to contain? Anything valuable would've been removed by the border guards during their searches.

Kurt lifted the clothes out and held up a shirt on the top. He recognised the brand. It was an expensive shirt — so Karl Rosenberg had been fairly wealthy, like his own family. He felt a kinship with the unknown boy and despite the unremarkable contents of the suitcase, he longed to return them and more importantly, to make contact with him. Perhaps they could be friends. Perhaps if they looked back far enough, they might even be related.

Kurt carried on removing everything and found at the bottom of the case, several sheets of paper. On one was a pencil drawing of a heart, cleverly designed with a bass clef forming one side of the shape and a treble clef inside, near the black and white keys of a piano. Next to the design, Karl — presumably it was Karl who'd drawn the heart — had written *Miriam* in loopy handwriting.

So Karl Rosenberg, was sweet on a girl called Miriam! He continued to look through the papers — just designs and scribbles but there on the last one, were two addresses, written in the same handwriting. One was for Ridley and Perkins Solicitors, who were situated in London W1. Kurt had no idea where that was. And the other address seemed to be the private home of Max Cavendish, although there was no clue who this person might be to Karl. Mr Cavendish also lived in London, although the address was St James's Square, London SW1.

Were the two places close? For the first time, Kurt was aware of how little he knew about his new home. Jack had called it the East End and he knew the shop was in Commercial Road, which apparently contained many other tailors, but there was going to be so much to learn.

He thought of Katya, unable to speak English, and wondered how she was faring. And the mournful girl whose name might have been Brigitte or Brunhilde, had she stopped crying?

Kurt placed everything back in the case, as he'd found it, except the sheet with the names and addresses which he tucked into his own case. Then he placed Karl's case under his own in an attempt to deter any of the Rayment boys from opening it. Not that he thought they were dishonest but they all had a pinched, hungry look about them and darting eyes as if they were searching for the next opportunity.

Opportunity for what, Kurt had no idea — but he didn't want Karl's belongings tampered with. Not while they were in his care.

* * *

Kurt had been so sad at leaving his mother and sisters, he hadn't given much thought to what he'd do in England. If someone had asked him, he'd probably have said life would be much the same for him in London as it had been in Berlin, except for living away from his family.

He'd go to school and in time, train to be a teacher; perhaps even a professor like his father. Then, when he was earning wages, he'd save up until he had enough to go back to Germany, find his father and bring his whole family to England.

Now, faced with the poverty of the Rayment family, he knew he would simply work and contribute his wages for his keep. There was only a certain amount of food and the more people in the house, the less everyone had to eat. And very soon, there would be yet another child to feed.

When Kurt expressed his wish to find a job, Jack said he'd like Kurt to work for him. Not for payment, but for his keep. The last worker Jack had employed had died of typhus a few months before. He'd tried to carry on alone but, as he pointed out, he couldn't be in two places at once.

Jack had trained as a tailor and boasted that his repairs and alterations were almost invisible and that he could make a bespoke suit like no one else in London — perhaps England. However, he couldn't afford enough quality cloth to make suits to display in the window, and risk them standing for months fading in the sunshine. Without being able to show his skills, no one called on him for anything other than simple repairs.

Most of his business involved selling mended and altered second-hand clothing which he bought from the many merchants in the area. He also purchased suits which had been damaged or outgrown, and once the seams were unpicked, he was often able to make a new pair of trousers or a jacket. Occasionally, if the suit had been large, there was enough to make a matching jacket and trousers.

But the skilful part of Jack's job was the cutting and sewing. Since his worker had died, it had fallen on him to go out and do the rounds of the second-hand clothing stores buying anything that would be useful, which meant he had little time to turn the clothes into something he could sell. Sylvia did the rounds when she could but she'd been ill throughout her pregnancy.

His three sons were still at school and although they accompanied their father from time to time and had a good idea of the sort of clothing he needed, Jack was adamant they remain at school at least until they reached fourteen.

After accompanying Jack to the various secondhand clothing and rag shops for a few days, Kurt went out on his own, doing the rounds on Jack's dilapidated bicycle. Occasionally, he made a delivery of a garment Jack had completed.

At first, Kurt found it difficult to understand the broad Cockney accent and because of the way his mother had taught him to speak English, he was teased and called 'Jack's little toff'.

Gradually, however, his good manners earned him respect. Several of the old ladies took a liking to him and put pieces to one side which they thought he might want — perhaps garments with expensive, fancy buttons which could be re-used, or a generously-sized suit.

The money Kurt had given Jack when he arrived had been used to purchase a better sewing machine. It was second-hand but it replaced one which was falling to pieces. Jack worked on the new machine while Sylvia used the old one to do much simpler sewing.

'There's something golden waiting for us, just around the corner, I feel it in my bones,' Jack would said periodically when he thought the family's fortunes were about to change for the better. This was usually followed by a slight shake of Sylvia's head and the lowering of her gaze as if she couldn't believe her husband's unbridled optimism in the face of their poverty.

Despite her doubts, the finances improved slightly since Jack had bought the new machine.

Jack knew someone who could take care of the paperwork for the change in Kurt's surname to Rayment and for his naturalisation. Although Kurt was very unhappy that his father's name would be lost, he could see how important it was to Jack that he become British. Nevertheless, it felt like a betrayal to the father who might even now have died in the concentration camp.

Mother wrote often, telling him about things that Inge had said or Renate had done but there was no news about Father. That meant she hadn't heard anything. She didn't tell him how they were living but from the newspaper reports, Kurt knew it was hard in Berlin for those Jews who remained. He longed to earn enough to get them out of Germany, but until Mother knew there was no hope of Father coming home, he realised she wouldn't leave their apartment.

* * *

One day, Kurt was about to set off on a delivery with a parcel wrapped in brown paper in his bicycle basket when he was stopped by Mr Penhaligon from the bookshop next door.

'You're not going near the hospital, are you?' he asked. 'One of the doctors who works there was asking about a book and I've finally tracked down a copy. If you're going near, you could deliver it. The price is inside. I'll pay you for your trouble.'

Kurt loved looking through the books in Mr Penhaligon's shop and enjoyed discussing current affairs with him. *Father would have liked Mr Penhaligon*, he thought, aware that he no longer had to suppress the German Vater and Mutti. After Jack's frequent warnings to act as though he was English born and bred, the words Father and Mother came quite naturally.

Kurt would have been happy to take the book to the hospital at Whitechapel, just a few blocks away, without payment but he knew Jack would be cross if he turned down a few pennies extra. So he took the book and placed it in his basket, promising to deliver it and to take payment.

On his return, Mr Penhaligon took the money and counted out a few pennies for Kurt.

'I've got something else I need to be delivered but it's further afield. I'd go myself but my knees are playing me up. When the weather is drier and warmer, my joints might be less painful. I don't suppose you ever go as far as the City, do you?'

'Which city?' Kurt asked in surprise.

Mr Penhaligon laughed. 'The City of London. The Square Mile. It's the financial district of London and the most historic. It's just up the road. Not a place you ever get to? Never mind. I thought it might be a bit far afield for Mr Rayment.'

'Is it very far?' Kurt asked with interest.

'Not for someone with a bicycle and strong, young legs like yours. I could lend you a map, if that would help. I'd pay extra, of course. But I wouldn't want to annoy Mr Rayment by keeping you from his business.'

A map! Perhaps it would cover the area where Ridley and Perkins Solicitors were and Kurt would be able to hand the suitcase in.

The following Wednesday afternoon after he'd finished working for Jack, he put the suitcase in his basket along with Mr Penhaligon's map and the book, which he delivered to the reception of a large bank not far from the Monument.

Then he cycled to Oxford Street. It occurred to him that since Rayment Tailors shut on Wednesday afternoon,

Ridley and Perkins Solicitors might also be closed but in the City of London, everything seemed to be very busy.

Every so often, there was so much traffic, he got off his bicycle and pushed it along through the crowds of bowler-hatted gentlemen and office workers. Finally, he turned down the quieter alley where Ridley and Perkins Solicitors were located.

The sign in the window showed the office was closed. Envelopes were sticking out of the letterbox, indicating that no one had been there for some time. Next to the closed sign was a sheet of paper with faded writing informing any potential clients that Ridley and Perkins had moved premises. It gave the new address and telephone number which Kurt wrote down although when he checked his map, he could see it was past Hammersmith, which seemed to be too far for him to attempt that day on his bicycle. He wondered whether to call them from a telephone box but he didn't want to spend the money and it wouldn't help him deliver the case.

St James's Square wasn't far and he decided to try there. With any luck, Mr Max Cavendish would take the suitcase and reunite it with its true owner.

2

Eleanor took her school hat off and pushed it into the depths of her school bag amongst her books. She was nearly home, and none of the teachers would spot her bare head now.

Flicking her blonde plaits over her shoulders, she transferred the heavy bag to the other hand.

Wednesday evening was always a bad night for homework and tonight was going to be worse than most, judging by the weight of books she'd brought home.

This evening, she had Latin spellings to learn and an essay to finish off for the English mistress.

But no history. Miss Vaughan, the history teacher, didn't believe in home-work. Not the written kind, anyway. She urged her girls to go to museums and libraries and to research the subjects they were studying — not just copy large chunks of text out of books, like some teachers.

Miss Vaughan invariably did things differently and somehow, she always seemed to get away with it, despite the school policy being that homework should be set. Miss Woods, the headmistress, was very strict but even so, the history teacher seemed to do what she liked.

Miss Vaughan had been a Suffragette — a very active Suffragette, who'd been imprisoned more than once and even suffered the indignity of being force-fed when she'd gone on hunger strike.

Some of the girls said it was because the headmistress was frightened of Miss Vaughan and her fierce reputation but Eleanor thought it more likely that Miss Woods respected what she'd done for womanhood. Yes, Miss Vaughan was a legend. All the girls adored her.

Eleanor thought that if Miss Vaughan were to walk around the corner now and spot her without her school hat on, she'd be pleased that Eleanor had shown spirit. That was something she always encouraged in her girls.

'Never let anyone crush your spirit, girls!' she said. Although Eleanor wasn't sure if being made to wear school uniform, especially the dreaded hat, counted as having her spirit crushed. And she suspected Miss Vaughan wouldn't approve of defiance for the sake of being defiant. But it would be her seventeenth birthday soon and Eleanor felt as if she ought to be different — older, wiser.

Mummy and Daddy still treated her as if she was a child. Well, not Daddy so much because, as a vice-admiral in the Royal Navy, he was rarely home. But when he was there, he still thought of her as a little girl. So, from time to time, she deliberately didn't do as she was told — on a matter of principle — and to her surprise, she often got away with it.

This afternoon, for example, she intended to go into the gardens in the centre of the square and sit for a while. Not because she wanted to, but because Mummy had told her not to go into the gardens on her own. But on Wednesday afternoons, Mummy played bridge with her friends and wouldn't be home for another few hours.

She was just about to cross the road to the entrance of the gardens in the middle of the square when she heard a raised voice. It was coming from next door to her parents' house.

Rigsby, the next-door neighbours' butler, was loudly telling a boy to go to the tradesman's entrance at the rear of the property.

'But I'm not trying to sell you anything,' the boy said. 'I'm trying to return this.'

The butler looked down his nose at the tatty, leather suitcase the boy held out.

'And I'm telling you, you guttersnipe, if you want to be seen, go to the tradesman's entrance!'

The boy placed the case on the

doorstep and turned. He walked quickly down the steps but just as he'd reached the pavement, Rigsby swung his leg back, then kicked the case high into the air where it spun and fell to the pavement. The impact caused both catches to break and the lid to fly open, spilling clothes on to the road.

For a second, the boy looked down in horror and then, leaning his bicycle against the railings, he stooped to pick up the scattered clothes.

Eleanor ran across the road and crouched down beside him to help.

'I wasn't trying to sell anything,' the boy said with a frown. 'He must have misunderstood.'

'I think Rigsby was absolutely beastly,' Eleanor said indignantly. 'Just look at your things, all over the ground!'

'Oh, they're not mine,' the boy said. 'I was trying to return them.'

'To Rigsby?'

'Well, no, I was trying to find out whether Karl Rosenberg was there. It's his suitcase, you see.'

'Is he a friend of yours?'

'No, I've never met him. But I've got his case.'

'Heavens! How intriguing! How did you get it?'

'It's quite a long story . . . '

The boy packed everything back in the case and jammed it inside his bicycle basket to keep the lid closed, now the clasps were broken.

Eleanor didn't want him to simply go. While she'd been crouching next to him, she'd noticed his dark eyes which were fringed with long, black lashes and she'd been fascinated. She'd never seen anyone with eyes quite like it and she wanted to look at them for longer.

'I've got time,' she said, wondering at her own boldness. 'Have you?'

'Well . . . '

'We could go into the garden,' she said. 'I was going in there anyway.'

He smiled. 'That would be nice.'

Eleanor threw glances at him as he walked beside her, pushing his bicycle. He was as tall as her but quite thin, and his cheekbones stood out starkly. But his most amazing feature was those mysterious eyes.

They sat together on a bench and he told her about life in Berlin with his parents and sisters, then about how their lives had changed once the Nazis rose in power and popularity.

'Miss Vaughan mentioned the Kindertransport children,' she said when he described his journey and how the suitcase came into his possession. 'And you think it belongs to someone who lives next door to me?'

'Well, I did because of the address in the case but if the butler didn't recognise the name, now I'm not so sure.'

The nearby church bells rang and Eleanor checked her watch. She knew it wouldn't be long until Mummy returned from bridge, but talking to Kurt was so exciting. Not only because she knew she shouldn't talk to strangers, but also because he made her feel so breathless.

I could sit and stare into his eyes

forever, she thought.

But soon he would be gone and she'd never see him again — unless she thought of something quickly. And then she had it.

'I could try to find out if the Cavendishes know anything about Karl, if you'd like,' she said, 'but how could I let you know? Would you be able to come back?'

'I could come on Sunday. Would that be all right?'

'Of course,' she said, determined she would either somehow miss the morning church service or the usual interminable, boring Sunday lunch. Whatever it took to meet Kurt again.

'What time could you make?' she asked.

'Possibly eleven o'clock,' he said uncertainly, 'it depends on . . . well, it just depends. But I'll try.'

She led him back to the garden entrance and expected him to ride away but instead, to her delight, he accompanied her to her house.

'Thank you for taking an interest,' he said.

'You're very welcome and when I ask Mrs Cavendish about Karl, I shall be sure to . . . ' she looked from right to left and lowering her voice, she leaned towards Kurt to whisper, 'tell her about how absolutely beastly Rigsby was to you.'

It was at that point that, over Kurt's shoulder, she saw the curtains of the drawing room twitch and her mother appear at the window.

'Heavens!' said Eleanor, leaping backwards away from Kurt, her cheeks beginning to glow red. 'I'm sorry, I must go!'

She took the steps two at a time. As she got the door, her mother opened it but she slipped inside, blocking the way. If Mummy saw Kurt on the pavement, she'd be bound to make a scene.

'Who were you talking to?' Mummy demanded.

'No one!'

'You were talking to a boy, I saw you!'

'Oh him,' Eleanor said airily. 'I've no

idea. He was asking me the way to Piccadilly Circus.'

'Piccadilly Circus? What nonsense! Now get out of my way!' She pushed past her daughter and rushed outside. Eleanor held her breath and closed her eyes, hoping desperately that Kurt had gone. There was no angry cry from her mother, so presumably, he'd already cycled off.

'And where have you been?' Mummy asked as she came back in to the elegant hall, checking her wrist watch.

'I stayed on a bit later at school,' lied Eleanor. 'Honestly, Mummy, I don't know what all the fuss is about.'

In the absence of any evidence to the contrary, she had to believe her daughter. She turned to go back in the drawing room.

Eleanor casually asked why her mother wasn't at bridge.

'Elspeth had one of her headaches, so it was cancelled. I'd have hosted it here but I'd already given cook the afternoon off.'

'Oh, that's a shame,' Eleanor said, hoping that Elspeth wouldn't suffer another headache on a Wednesday.

She turned with a sigh and walked up the stairs to her bedroom. Defiance was very exciting when everything went right, but hard work when things went wrong.

That night, Eleanor lay in bed remembering Kurt and the feeling in the pit of her stomach when she looked into his eyes. Hopefully, she'd see him at eleven o'clock on Sunday. Mummy didn't go to church, but she always sent Eleanor. It wouldn't be too difficult to slip away and go to the garden to meet Kurt.

Tomorrow, she'd have to try to find out whether the Cavendishes had a house guest called Karl Rosenberg and if he'd lost a suitcase. She wasn't bothered either way. All that mattered was that Kurt was going to come on Sunday and that she'd see him again.

* * *

Kurt couldn't understand it. One minute Eleanor was leaning in towards him and the next, she'd seen something over his shoulder, gasped in horror and run off.

He'd looked behind him at the grand Georgian house for some clue as to why she'd fled, but there was no sign. Alarmed by her reaction, he'd mounted his bicycle and quickly ridden away without looking back.

Sometime later, he stopped outside a shop to get his breath back and caught sight of his reflection in the window. He'd lost weight since he'd left Germany and his clothes now hung on his thin frame. His trousers were slightly too short, his hair far too long and beginning to curl.

Kurt decided he'd have to scrape together money to go to the barbers. He'd seen Sylvia cut the boys' hair but she'd merely put a bowl on each child's head and trimmed around the bottom.

He felt ridiculous and embarrassed that he looked so scruffy. What on earth must that girl have made of him? He'd have to smarten up somehow if he was going to meet her on Sunday.

If he was going to meet her? Of course he was going to meet her! He couldn't wait for Sunday.

He cycled home, entered the yard at the back of the shop and leaned his bicycle against the wall. There was a strong smell of vinegar from the house and he wondered what Sylvia was cooking for tea. When he entered the kitchen, he saw the three boys sitting on stools, their hair wet. Sylvia was leaning over Benjamin, combing his hair.

'Lice,' she said, seeing Kurt looking puzzled. 'We'll have to do you too,' she said without enthusiasm. 'Paraffin's better for treating them but I can't afford to waste it, so it'll have to be vinegar and we'll keep our fingers crossed.'

She passed him a bowl of vinegar and told him to wet his hair.

Kurt shivered with disgust. His skin crawled at the thought of tiny creatures living in his hair. His head had started to itch but he hadn't paid any attention, not having had any reason to consider head lice before.

'Can you cut my hair?' Kurt asked, desperate to get rid of all trace of the insects and their eggs.

'Jack's gone to Mr Friedman the barber to see if he'll come down and use the clippers on the boys,' Sylvia said. 'He can do you too, if you like.'

That night when Kurt went to bed, the smell of vinegar was still in his nostrils and his head felt cold where his hair had been cut close to his scalp. There were no more nits or lice but he fancied he could feel them. Then he had a such a dreadful thought he sat up, forgetting the sloping ceiling above his bed and striking his head.

Eleanor hadn't been looking over his shoulder when she suddenly looked aghast. She'd been looking *at* him — at the lice in his hair. It had been when she leaned in towards him that she'd suddenly appeared horrified and run away.

Hot tears of humiliation pricked at his eyelids. There was no question of him going to meet her on Sunday. After spotting he was lousy, she wouldn't consider ever meeting him again.

Sleep eluded him and he lay watching the moon through the tiny attic window. How he wished he could simply fly out into the night sky and be lost among the stars. He was grateful to Jack and Sylvia for taking him in, of course, but what had once seemed like a temporary measure had taken on a more permanent outlook because there were no alternatives.

Kurt was trapped. He'd lost his country, his family, his surname — and his hair and his dignity.

Once upon a time, he'd have been able to meet Eleanor on an equal social footing. Perhaps his family wasn't quite as rich as hers — her house was larger and grander — but he could have held his head up as the son of distinguished Professor Rosenberg.

Now, he lodged with a family who

despite Jack's good intentions and hard work, was barely making a living. Any day now the baby would be born, putting further strain on the finances.

He would work twice as hard. He would see if Mr Penhaligon could give him more work. But deep down, he knew it was useless. There would need to be twice as many hours in a day for him to make enough money to help the Rayments and allow him to assist his own family in Germany.

In the street, the muffled sound of piano music and raucous voices suddenly grew louder as if someone had opened a door. The sound came from the Princess Alice pub on the corner. A woman laughed shrilly, and for the first time, Kurt realised what attracted so many to the pub in the evening. It catered for those who'd realised that, like him, they would never get out of the poverty in which they found themselves and the only respite could be found at the bottom of a glass of gin.

By the time he went to sleep that

night, the moon had passed out of his view through the tiny window but the yearning remained to fly away.

* * *

'Eleanor Taylor-Scott! Have you been listening to anything I've been saying this lesson?' Miss Vaughan said crossly. 'What is so interesting that you can't take your eyes off the window?'

'Oh, nothing, Miss Vaughan!' Eleanor said in alarm.

'Well, see me after the lesson is over.'

Eleanor waited until the other girls had left and then slowly walked to Miss Vaughan's desk with her head lowered. Miss Vaughan was the last person she wanted to anger.

'Your behaviour is rather out of character, Eleanor. Is there a reason for your lack of interest in today's lesson?'

Eleanor considered telling the teacher about meeting Kurt but decided against it. Adults could be very unpredictable. And her favourite teacher thought crushes on boys were utterly frivolous.

'Oh, no, Miss Vaughan. I'm sorry, it won't happen again.'

'If there's something troubling you, Eleanor . . . ?'

'Oh, no, Miss. I'm fine, thanks. I just didn't sleep very well last night.'

When Miss Vaughan finally allowed her to go, Harriet, her best friend was waiting for her.

'Did she give you lines?' she asked.

'No, thankfully.'

'Well, don't push your luck in the next lesson. Mrs Wilson'll keep you in after school if you don't look like you're paying attention. What's the matter? You've been miles away all morning.'

'Nothing,' said Eleanor, unable to suppress a smile.

'Come on, tell me! You're keeping a secret!'

'All right, but promise not to tell.'

'Cross my heart.'

'I met a boy yesterday. He's so handsome. And I'm going to see him again on Sunday.'

‘Where d’you meet him?’

‘Well, sort of next door.’

‘In the Cavendishes’ house?’

‘Not exactly. More outside their house really.’

‘Tell me everything!’

Eleanor explained about Kurt and how they’d spent time in the garden while he told her about his home in Germany.

‘So, where does he live now?’ Harriet asked.

‘I don’t know. I didn’t ask and he didn’t say but he had a bicycle, so it probably wasn’t very close. I’ll ask him on Sunday. Oh, Harriet, he has such beautiful eyes!’

‘So, how will you find out whether the boy he’s looking for is staying with the Cavendishes?’

‘I don’t know. I can’t just knock and ask to see Mrs Cavendish without a good reason. She’s rather fierce. And of course, I can’t ask Mummy to enquire. I’ve been wondering how all day. That’s what I was thinking about in Miss

Vaughan's lesson — well, that and how gorgeous Kurt is.'

'I might have a way,' said Harriet. 'Mrs Cavendish's niece is in Louisa's class.'

Louisa was Harriet's younger sister.

'D'you know who she is?' Eleanor asked, eager to find the girl and ask her if she knew anything about Karl Rosenberg.

It was almost the end of lunchtime before Harriet located Louisa, and asked her to find the girl they were looking for. Louisa finally pointed out a timid girl hovering near a group of her classmates.

'Geraldine Martin?' Harriet asked.

The girl jumped and blushed as she realised that two of the older girls wanted to talk to her and that her classmates had stopped chatting and were staring at her.

'I wonder if you could help us please,' Harriet said politely and the girls watched open-mouthed as Geraldine followed Harriet and Eleanor.

Geraldine often visited the Cavendishes. She told Eleanor they'd been expecting a young German refugee to stay with them but although he'd arrived in London safely, he'd decided to stay with a family friend in Hatton Garden instead. She couldn't remember his name but she thought it might well have been Karl Rosenberg.

As Eleanor and Harriet thanked her and left, the other girls gathered around the suddenly-popular Geraldine and demanded to know why she'd been sought out by the older girls.

'See,' said Harriet, with a laugh, 'I could've saved you all that trouble with Miss Vaughan earlier, if you'd told me you had a problem.'

'You can't make the time pass faster until Sunday, can you? I'm not sure how I'm going to get through the rest of today and then Saturday.'

'There's a limit to even my powers, I'm afraid,' Harriet said, linking arms with Eleanor on the way to their next lesson.

* * *

It was drizzling when Eleanor woke on Sunday morning and when she saw the rain on the window, her heart sank. Mummy would be sure to tell Rodgers to prepare the car to take her daughter to St James's Church. It was only a short walk but Mummy wouldn't see the sense in getting wet and that would mean Eleanor wouldn't be able to go to the garden to wait for Kurt.

By the time Eleanor had finished breakfast, the rain had stopped. Daddy was away for the weekend and Mummy still hadn't got up, so she left the house quietly and with a glance to make sure no one was watching from the window, she made her way to the garden.

Still half an hour to wait until Kurt came.

If he came.

He simply must come. She wouldn't be able to bear it if he didn't.

The church bells rang out eleven o'clock but there was no sign of Kurt. It began to rain but still Eleanor lingered by the statue of William III until midday. Then, thoroughly drenched and downhearted, she went home.

Sunday lunch was a quiet affair. Her mother was nursing a hangover and seemed almost relieved that Eleanor was quiet.

By the evening, Eleanor had given herself a good talking-to. How stupid she'd been to have spent so much time thinking about a boy she'd met on the street and spoken to for such a short time. He'd obviously had no intention of coming to St James's Square today.

* * *

On Monday morning, Harriet rushed over to Eleanor when she arrived at school.

'Did he come?'

Eleanor shook her head.

'Never mind,' said the ever-practical Harriet, 'you wouldn't have been able to hide it from your mother for long and when she found out you'd been seeing a boy behind her back, you'd never have been allowed out on your own again.'

'No, I suppose not.'

'Your mother's like mine, she'll want you to make a good match, so mixing with anyone she doesn't know won't be allowed. I think my mother already has someone in mind.'

'Really? Who?'

'The son of one of Daddy's business partners.'

'Really?'

'Yes. I've known him since I was very young. I don't want to marry him and I'm certain he doesn't want to marry me. He's such a bore. And he's only interested in cars.'

'So what are you going to do?'

'Nothing. Just make it look like I'm going along with Mummy's plans. It's easiest. When I'm a bit older, I'll get a job and do as I please.'

Eleanor was impressed that Harriet had thought things through that far.

'A job? But won't your mother stop you?'

'She'll try. But I shall simply run away. I've been saving up and I think I can survive on my own for long enough to find a job and a room somewhere.'

'What will you do?'

'Get a job in an office. I'd like to be a journalist, so I'll try the newspaper offices first but if they don't want me, I'll be able to get a job elsewhere.

'I don't think it'll come to that. Mummy will give in, I know she will. But if she doesn't, Daddy will send me money.'

Eleanor thought about that conversation all the way home after school. How could it be that her best friend, Harriet, had made so many plans about her future — even considering a contingency, should her first plans go wrong, and yet, Eleanor hadn't considered her own future? She'd been so busy living in the moment, and assuming her parents would manage her life — just as they'd done since she'd been born. It hadn't occurred to her that she should be making her own plans.

Her parents were not as easy-going as Harriet's. Her mother would not accept Eleanor working in an office. She knew this because at one of the meetings between her teachers and parents, her English mistress had suggested that since Eleanor was such a tidy and organised girl, she might be suited to secretarial work. Mother had quickly corrected her and said it would be a waste of Eleanor's time working in an office.

The teacher had not argued but on the way home, Eleanor asked what she would be doing instead.

'Why, running your own home, that's what! Not doing menial tasks for a boss. And of course, in the fullness of time, becoming a mother.'

That had been that. It had been so far in the future that Eleanor hadn't bothered much. But, she realised with a start, the time had almost come. Worse, if she didn't have an idea of what she wanted to do, Mummy would decide for her. In all probability Mummy would want to decide anyway. Eleanor needed an emergency plan.

That evening during dinner with her parents, she broached the subject.

'One of my teachers was telling us about applying for university today,' she said.

No one had mentioned it that day but it had certainly been spoken about before and the girls had been encouraged to consider the option.

'Well, you're not thinking about it, are you, Eleanor?' her mother said with the confidence of someone who always knew exactly what her daughter was thinking.

'Well . . . I was wondering about leaving school and perhaps . . . getting a job . . . of some sort.'

'A job? Whatever for?' Mummy said.

'Well, to earn some money . . . '

'You don't need to worry your pretty little head about money,' Daddy said. 'Have you spent your allowance this month already?'

'No, Daddy. I haven't spent it but I thought it might be nice to earn my own money.'

'Darling,' said Mummy patiently, 'you don't need to worry about money. Your father more than provides for all our needs.' She waved her arms about to indicate their large, sumptuously decorated dining room, silver cutlery and bone china. 'And one day soon your husband will do the same. Assuming you choose wisely, of course.'

'You make it sound like buying a coat.'

'Don't be so ridiculous, darling! It'll be the most important decision you'll make.'

'But suppose I can't find someone I like?'

'Of course you will. There are plenty of eligible men out there.'

'Unless of course, we have another war, Alice,' Daddy said to Mummy.

'You aren't helping, Ernest!'

'But, Mummy, you're assuming I want to get married,' Eleanor said.

Her mother placed her cutlery on her plate, dabbed the corners of her mouth with her serviette and turned her full attention on her daughter.

'There is no question you will get married. How else will you make your way in the world?'

'Get a job?'

'Eleanor! You're being impossible! I refuse to discuss this important topic with you while you're behaving like a child! You may leave school if that's what you wish. But you will not waste your time working in a silly job. And one day, you will get married. If you don't, you'll regret it.'

Later, Eleanor ran the conversation over and over in her mind. So her life had been mapped out. But Mummy wasn't right about one thing. Miss Vaughan had never married and she said she was perfectly happy. What's more, she'd led a really exciting, fulfilling life. Eleanor decided she would find Miss Vaughan the following day at school and ask her opinion.

* * *

'Only you can decide how you want to spend the rest of your life, Eleanor,' Miss Vaughan said.

'But my parents seem to have worked out exactly what's going to happen and I don't think I've got any say.'

'Well, far be it for me to encourage you to disobey your parents, but you are the one who's going to be living your life. It'll be you who enjoys the benefits and you who pays for the mistakes, so it should be you who makes the decisions.'

Eleanor nodded and sighed.

'Mummy won't hear anything about me getting a job. She says it's a waste of time and that I'd be better off putting my efforts into finding a husband. If, one day, the right person comes along, I wouldn't mind but I'd like to do something first and see a bit of the world. Like you did.'

'Well, I'm not sure my life would be suited to everyone. And of course, now, there's no need for all that struggle and strife. Women have won the right to vote. But I believe there's a war coming and if it does, then life will be very different. And just like in the last war, women's roles will be of much greater significance.'

'Do you really think there'll be a war?'

'Yes, sadly. Our government can turn its back for so long but ultimately, it'll have to do something to help our European neighbours.'

Eleanor had come away feeling very despondent. Miss Vaughan always seemed to have the answer to everything but it was probably too much to expect her to sort out Eleanor's life.

As she'd said, it was up to Eleanor. And as for there being a war . . . Daddy had mentioned it several times during the last few months but then he was in the Royal Navy, so thoughts of fighting and conflict were part of his job. And whenever he began to speak of the possibility of war, Mummy always stopped him.

The previous September, Prime Minister Neville Chamberlain had returned from a meeting with Adolf Hitler in Germany, claiming to have negotiated 'peace with honour' declaring that he believed there would be 'peace in our time'.

Surely he couldn't be wrong?

Eleanor felt as though she'd been wearing blinkers and they'd suddenly been removed. So many things she'd known about, but hadn't taken notice of, came sharply into focus. She started to read Daddy's newspapers and to listen to news reports on the wireless. How could she have been so unaware of real life? It seemed that school work and the occasional trip to Selfridges and other stores with Mummy to buy clothes had filled her world. Now, she thirsted to understand what was going on around her.

Eleanor knew her mother was stubborn and that if she wanted to go against her wishes, she was going to have to be determined and resourceful.

Surprisingly, she realised she could be as obstinate and as headstrong as her mother and that sooner or later, they were going to clash.

Nevertheless, Eleanor was resolute. She was going to leave school in the summer and find a job in an office. If Mother didn't like it, she'd have to put up with it. And if she wouldn't? Well, perhaps Eleanor would share a room with Harriet, once they were both earning.

* * *

1939

During the summer, the Taylor-Scott family went to Scotland to stay on Daddy's brother's estate, so Eleanor didn't have a chance to look for a job after she'd left school.

It was pleasant in Scotland with her aunt and uncle. Although the social life wasn't quite as hectic as in London, Eleanor enjoyed the tennis parties, picnics and dances.

However, she had the disturbing feeling that she was merely marking time, and when Harriet's letter arrived, informing her she'd managed to get a job at The Times newspaper and was renting a small room, Eleanor longed to go home.

Harriet said she'd asked about the possibility of Eleanor getting a job there and although they didn't need anyone at the moment, they'd make a note that Harriet's friend was available.

There was also the prospect of war. Uncle Hector said that the Prime Minister had negotiated peace with Hitler and somehow, Britain would keep out of the conflict. Aunt Millicent wouldn't discuss the possibility and neither would Mummy. Daddy spent lots of time in Uncle Hector's study on the telephone to the Admiralty and he usually emerged frowning, although he didn't divulge the content of the conversations to anyone.

The air of anxiety that Eleanor and her parents had left behind in London hadn't reached Uncle Hector's estate, although from time to time, the young people Eleanor met at parties discussed politics. Generally it was believed that Britain would be at war before the end of 1939.

One morning in early August, Daddy received a call from the Admiralty which resulted in him packing his bags and leaving for Portsmouth. Mummy and Eleanor continued their holiday without him but not long after, Mummy started to get bored. Eleanor recognised the signs and knew she was missing the hustle and bustle of London and her regular bridge parties.

Eventually, her mother made her excuses, thanked Uncle Hector and Aunt Millicent profusely for their hospitality, then she and Eleanor caught the train back to London.

They arrived home six days before they'd been due to return, taking the staff by surprise. Unwin, the butler, said that the Vice Admiral had taken a suite in Claridges, presumably until his wife and daughter returned, so Mummy suggested they go to the hotel for dinner and to surprise Daddy.

As a waiter led them towards a table for two in the Art Deco restaurant, Mrs Taylor-Scott spotted a friend and her son sitting by one of the large arch-topped windows.

'Oh, look, darling, there's Phyllis Ardley and her son, Geoffrey. Let's go and say hello.'

'I thought we were having dinner with Daddy.'

'I haven't been able to get hold of him. Apparently, he's out of his office, so I've left a note at reception. But in the meantime, it'd be rude not to sit with Phyllis and Geoffrey.'

The waiter pulled another table and chairs up to the Ardleys, so they could all sit together.

Surely Mummy didn't believe Eleanor was unaware of her efforts to throw her together with eligible young men? She'd spent much of their time in Scotland trying to ensure Eleanor was invited to every social event in the area. Now it seemed she'd contrived this meeting in Claridges.

If it hadn't been so annoying, Eleanor would have laughed. She'd met Geoffrey before and he was a pleasant young man, but she didn't have the slightest interest in him. But Eleanor would play along as if she was totally unaware of her mother's efforts to matchmake.

'Oh, Alice, darling, I've got such good news!' Phyllis said when the newcomers were seated.

'Mummy!' Geoffrey said with annoyance. 'Catherine and I wanted to keep it quiet until she's been able to contact her parents in India.'

'Oh, Geoffrey, Alice and Eleanor won't tell anyone, will you, darlings?'

They assured Phyllis they wouldn't.

'See! Now please, let me tell them.'

Geoffrey sighed and frowned but agreed.

'Geoffrey and Catherine Falkes-Hyde are engaged! Well, what d'you think of that?'

'Lovely,' Mummy said and gave Eleanor an accusing look as if to say, *if you don't start trying to find a husband soon, you're going to miss out on all the best catches*. Obviously Mummy hadn't set up the meeting; it had simply been a coincidence they were all in the restaurant.

And then something happened which took away all thoughts of Mummy exerting pressure on Eleanor to find a husband.

On the far side of the restaurant, an elegant man entered with a tall, blonde woman on his arm. He held his hand over hers and as she turned towards him, he kissed her cheek.

The blood drained from Eleanor's face because the elegant man was her father.

Eleanor knew Mummy had seen her husband with the woman, although she said nothing. Phyllis, who had her back to Daddy, prattled about the party they would hold for Geoffrey's engagement and was so engrossed in her plans, she didn't notice that when the main course arrived, Mummy ate very little and pushed most of it around her place with her fork.

Her mother claimed to have developed a migraine when the waiter returned with the dessert menus and saying that she really had to go, she offered to pay for the entire meal, leaving Phyllis and Geoffrey to dessert and coffee.

'Telephone me tomorrow and let me know how you are, Alice, darling. And I wanted to ask your advice on outfits for the wedding . . . ' Phyllis said.

Mummy led Eleanor out of the far door, away from Daddy and the woman.

When they arrived home, Eleanor went to her bedroom. She was finding it hard to believe what she'd seen and was beginning to wonder if perhaps her father had a double. She might even have convinced herself of that if it hadn't been for Mummy's behaviour.

Hearing a voice in the hall, Eleanor

crept out of her bedroom on to the landing and heard her mother in the hall below, telephone Claridges and ask to speak to Vice Admiral Taylor-Scott who was currently dining in the restaurant.

'Yes, I'll wait,' she said and then there was a long pause as she tapped her fingernails on the hall table.

Finally, she said, 'Ernest!'

She paused while presumably Daddy greeted her, unaware his wife was in London and had seen him with another woman.

'Eleanor and I were in Claridges restaurant this evening.' Mummy paused allowing the information to sink in, then she carried on, 'I would appreciate it if you came home immediately.'

Why wasn't she shouting? Eleanor wondered. It was as if seeing her husband with another woman hadn't been a surprise — although she was obviously very disturbed.

Later, her father arrived home and once again, Eleanor crept out of her bedroom on to the landing and listened as her father put his suitcases on the hall floor. He'd obviously checked out of Claridges and returned home.

Mummy came out of the sitting room where she'd been waiting.

'Alice?' Daddy said, his voice uncertain.

'How dare you humiliate me like that! How could you have behaved so disgracefully with that . . . that *floozy* in public? And when your daughter was across the room . . .'

'Darling, I'm so sorry.'

'Don't 'darling' me! You promised you'd be discreet. You promised!'

The door slammed, and although Eleanor heard raised voices, she couldn't make out the words.

She crept back to bed. So it wasn't the first time her father had been unfaithful to her mother.

What was even more unbelievable was that her mother was trying to hasten Eleanor into marriage when her own was so imperfect.

She lay awake much of the night, her thoughts in turmoil. It had never occurred to her that her parents were anything other than happy together, so to see her father with another woman and to learn that her mother was aware of his affairs, had destroyed something inside her.

Before, she'd wondered if she was doing the right thing in disregarding her parents' advice — despite Miss Vaughan saying she had to take responsibility for her own life and despite Harriet having done just that. Now, she knew without doubt she had to make her own decisions. How could she trust her parents when they'd obviously made such a mess of their own lives?

It occurred to her that it wasn't so important knowing the right way to go, so long as you knew where you wanted to end up — and where you *didn't* want to end up. Once you knew that, then you just took it step by step until you got there.

Tomorrow, she'd make a list of all the

jobs that appealed to her and then apply for them.

She finally fell asleep feeling more settled than she'd done for a while.

* * *

The following morning, Eleanor got up to find the breakfast room empty. Her father had left early — before his newspaper arrived, so while Eleanor nibbled her toast, she scanned the Situations Vacant pages and noted down any office jobs which she thought would be suitable.

She'd seen the maid deliver a breakfast tray to Mummy's bedroom, so she knew she wouldn't be disturbed. After writing several letters of application for jobs, she washed and dressed, then walked to the postbox to post them.

She wanted to talk to Harriet to find out whether she had any more news about a job at The Times but it was Friday and she knew her friend would be at work. She decided that on Saturday morning, she'd get up early, go to a public telephone box and call her. Her parents might easily hear her conversation if she used the telephone at home and it was probably best not to antagonise them while the atmosphere was so strained.

She wasn't sure whether her parents had made up or were even talking. It wasn't unusual for her father to go out to work early and with the threat of Germany invading Poland, it was almost expected for him to be at his desk.

As for her mother — well, when she had a migraine, she often spent the day in bed. Not that Eleanor believed her mother was sick but of course after the shock of seeing her husband with another woman, it was possible she was unwell.

Whatever was going on, Eleanor didn't want to go home and she decided she'd go for a walk.

It might be a good idea to use this

time to travel to some of the offices she'd applied to and find out how easy it was to get there. She'd decided to save any money she had for when she moved out, so it seemed a waste to spend it on fares now but if she planned her route carefully, she could perhaps walk much of the way.

The farthest distant company she'd applied to was near St Paul's Cathedral, and she decided to go there on the bus and then walk to the next one which was near Holborn. After that, she'd see what the time was and how tired she was.

The roads were busy around St Paul's and it took her some time to find the company down a side street. It was a bookbinder, situated in a basement below a hardware store. She looked through the railings at the steps which led down to the office and with dismay, noticed the rubbish which had accumulated outside. A rat darted out of the filthy area and Eleanor decided if she was offered the job, she'd turn it down.

The next place on her list was near Holborn, so she set off walking through the crowds of people, feeling very out of place. She wondered if Harriet felt the same or if, now that she was working, she felt as though she belonged. Ahead of her were two young women both dressed in a blue uniform. They had their arms linked and seemed oblivious to the annoyed glances of the people who were trying to pass them.

Eleanor envied them. How self-assured they looked. How certain of their place in this busy London street. And how purposeful.

The two girls, still arm in arm, turned into a large building at the same time as three other girls, all dressed in the same blue uniform. Eleanor stopped and looked up at the sign — *Adastral House, Air Ministry*.

'Thinking of joining the WAAFs?' someone said from behind her. Eleanor swung round to see a ginger-haired girl wearing the same uniform.

'Yes,' Eleanor said with a certainty

that surprised her, 'I am. What do I have to do?'

'Come inside and see the recruiting officer. You won't regret it. Joining up's the best thing I ever did. It's hard work but you'll learn a trade. And it's great fun!'

* * *

'You'll receive a letter shortly inviting you for an interview if your application's successful,' the officer said, as Eleanor handed in her completed application form.

At last, she felt as though her life was about to become meaningful. At last, she would be contributing something. Miss Vaughan would be proud of her.

Her father didn't come home that night and her mother didn't appear for dinner, so Eleanor ate alone and went to bed early.

The following day, she telephoned Harriet from a public box and they arranged to meet up for lunch. 'I'll pay,'

Harriet said, 'but we can't go anywhere expensive.'

Harriet told her about her new job, learning shorthand and typing as well as accounting.

'I keep asking about a job for you,' she said, 'but there's nothing yet.'

'I might have something,' Eleanor said. 'I only applied yesterday but I should hear soon if I've got an interview.'

'Where? I hope it's nearby, then we can meet up for lunch.'

'If I get it, I've no idea where I'll be working. I'm joining the WAAF!'

'How exciting! What'll you do?'

'I don't know. I met a girl who's joined and she works in an office in the headquarters in Holborn, so I'll ask if I can do something like that.'

Harriet sighed. 'I wish I'd thought of that. Especially now Hitler's marching into Poland — there's bound to be a war.'

'Well, it's not too late. I only handed in my application yesterday. You could apply too.'

That evening, Harriet invited Eleanor to stay overnight. She telephoned her mother to say she'd be with Harriet, knowing she would assume it was her friend's parents' house and not a small room near Aldgate. Mummy sounded distracted, readily agreeing, and Eleanor was grateful not to be returning home to another evening on her own.

The following morning, the two girls got up late, having been talking until the early hours. Harriet turned the wireless on at eleven o'clock so they wouldn't miss the Prime Minister's broadcast from the BBC. At quarter past eleven, Neville Chamberlain began to speak in serious tones.

'I am speaking to you from the cabinet room at 10 Downing Street. This morning, the British Ambassador in Berlin handed the German government a final note stating that unless we heard from them by eleven o'clock that they were prepared at once to withdraw their troops from Poland, a state of war would exist between us. I have to tell you now that no such undertaking has been received and consequently, this country is at war with Germany.'

Eleanor and Harriet stared at each other over the box which served as a table.

'I don't believe it! We're at war. How can that be possible?' Harriet whispered.

Eleanor shook her head, unable to take in the magnitude of the Prime Minister's words.

Minutes later, the two girls were startled by the dreadful wailing of an air raid siren which rang out through the streets, bringing terrified people out of their buildings to gather on the pavement, looking up at the blue, September sky for German aircraft.

Harriet led Eleanor into the basement with the other tenants of the building. They huddled in the dank cold until the all clear sounded.

'Was it a false alarm?' a man asked as they filed up the steps out of the basement.

‘Or a practice drill,’ someone else suggested.

Eleanor wondered what her parents would be doing. Daddy would be at work. But Mummy? She hated the cellar, not liking the thought of spiders. Had she simply remained in bed?

Eleanor knew it was time to go home.

* * *

The declaration of war seemed to have shocked Mummy out of her apathy. No longer did she spend hours alone in her room, avoiding dinner with Eleanor and her father when he was able to come home from work.

She joined committees with her friends aimed at raising money for war work, providing necessary items for the troops such as socks and gloves, and ensuring that, should German bombs start dropping, everyone knew how to operate a stirrup pump to extinguish fires.

She urged her daughter to join her, or at least to get involved in some sort of voluntary work but Eleanor, who hovered anxiously in the hall each morning, waiting for a reply to her application to the WAAF, told her she was considering it and would make up her mind soon.

In the meantime, she helped organise the tidying of the basement to turn it into a habitable space, should they need to shelter from bombs. Eleanor had been correct — Mummy had simply ignored the air raid siren which sounded shortly after Neville Chamberlain's radio broadcast.

Blackout curtains were fitted throughout the house and each pane of glass was criss-crossed with tape to prevent them shattering. The maids were sent into the basement to clean thoroughly. Once they'd removed all cobwebs and washed everything down, Unwin organised for an electricity supply to be run down there. After cleaning, it still smelled damp and earthy but it was far cosier with chairs, beds and a table on an old rug. And, of course, the electric lights banished the gloomy corners where spiders might lurk.

Finally, the letter from the Air Ministry arrived and Eleanor snatched it from Unwin before he had a chance to take it with the other letters into the breakfast room. She ran upstairs and turning it over and over, wondered what she'd do if she wasn't invited for interview.

She'd received several requests to attend interviews for the jobs she'd applied for and the bookbinder near St Paul's Cathedral had offered her the post without have set eyes on her, but she'd turned them all down in the hope she'd be accepted into the WAAF. Now she wondered if she hadn't acted too rashly.

She slipped her finger under the flap of the envelope, tore across, then withdrew the letter.

She gasped and then whooped with delight. Her interview was at the end of September.

* * *

When the day came, she dressed carefully, trying to appear smart, businesslike and older than her seventeen years.

Harriet had also applied to join the WAAF but was still waiting to hear from the Air Ministry and Eleanor knew it was unlikely that if they were both admitted, that they would train together. She would just have to make new friends.

She recalled seeing the two WAAFs walking along Holborn, arms linked, and the friendly ginger-haired woman outside Adastral House. Since then, whenever she'd seen anyone in the attractive blue WAAF uniform, she'd noticed groups of girls chatting animatedly, almost like schoolgirls, except these young women had poise and confidence.

Eleanor caught an early bus and arrived half an hour before her interview, her stomach knotted with nerves. What would they ask her? More importantly, what would she reply?

By the time she was shown into the recruiting office, she was shaking. The sergeant was calm and professional and Eleanor began to feel more relaxed. It seemed to be going well.

'Now, Miss Taylor-Scott, what trade shall I put you down for?'

Eleanor's heart leapt. He hadn't added, *if we accept you*.

Feeling slightly more confident, she said, 'Well, sir, I had hoped to learn office skills . . .'

Without looking up, he said 'Cook,' and wrote as much on her form. She wondered if he'd misheard her but dared not ask.

She was sent for a medical examination and eye test before being returned to the sergeant.

He looked up as she was led back in.

'Well, congratulations, Miss Taylor-Scott. You'll receive your call-up papers, a travel warrant and instructions on where to report for your training within the next few days. Don't bring too much luggage and don't miss your train.'

She was in! Even if he hadn't taken notice of her request. Perhaps there'd be an opportunity to change trades once she'd started.

'Any questions?'

'One thing, sir. Would it be possible to drop the 'Scott' from my surname? It's such a mouthful.'

'Good idea,' he said and made a note on her form, then placing it in one of the wire trays on his desk, he rose and shook her hand.

'Welcome to the WAAF, Miss Taylor.'

Unusually that evening, her father was home and the three of them were together for dinner. Her parents were being cordial to each other at long last. Since war had been declared, her father was busy at work and her mother's war work seemed to give her direction and purpose.

Tonight, Eleanor must tell them.

She waited until the soup had been

served and the maid gone, before she began.

'Mummy and Daddy, I have some very important news . . . I've joined up. I've had my interview and I'll start training very soon.'

There was silence for a few moments and then her mother wailed.

'How could you have gone behind our backs like that, Eleanor? Whatever possessed you? But don't think you've had the last word. Ernest,' she said, looking at her husband, 'can't you pull some strings and get her out?'

'I definitely can,' Daddy said. 'First thing tomorrow, I'll get in touch with the recruitment people. If you want to do war work, why don't you join your mother's committees?'

'Exactly,' Mummy said, for the first time in a while, agreeing wholeheartedly with her husband. 'You have such a rosy future ahead of you, Eleanor. Not many girls have your privileges. Why are you trying to throw it all away? Don't think you'll find yourself an officer husband like that. You won't be allowed to mix with the officers. You'll be the lowest of the low.'

'I don't want to marry an officer. That wasn't the point,' said Eleanor. 'I don't want to get married at all. Not unless I meet someone special. But I want to do something meaningful with my life.'

'Well, you'll have to think again, my girl, because by tomorrow morning, Daddy will have overturned your acceptance.'

Eleanor rose slowly.

'I'm really sorry you're taking my news this way. I appreciate you both want the best for me but rushing me into marriage isn't what I want. And, Daddy, I shouldn't waste your time tomorrow. You both seem to have assumed I joined the Royal Navy. I've joined the Royal Air Force. I think you'll agree, you have no jurisdiction there.'

She walked from the dining room.

'Ernest?' Mummy said uncertainly as

if she expected her husband to do something. But as Eleanor shut the dining room door behind her, Daddy remained silent.

Tears came to Eleanor's eyes as she climbed the stairs. She'd been so excited by her news, she thought that after the initial shock they would be glad for her.

Perhaps they still might, she thought. But it seemed unlikely. Her mother's desire for her to get married seemed to override everything.

* * *

1939

Eleanor's call-up papers arrived at the end of October, informing her she was to report to RAF Abbsworth, Gloucestershire, for training on Monday, November the sixth.

Her parents had become reconciled to her decision and although her father hadn't actually said so, Eleanor thought he was rather proud.

Mummy nursed an air of martyrdom although on the morning Eleanor left, she insisted her daughter ate a good breakfast and took a packet of sandwiches for the journey.

Daddy pressed a ten-pound note into her hand. He didn't say anything but his eyes were moist.

'Thank you, Daddy.'

He nodded. 'If you change your mind . . . '

'I won't, Daddy.'

'Telephone me when you arrive,' Mummy said tearfully as Eleanor set off with her suitcase and gas mask. 'I love you, darling,' she called out as Eleanor walked down the steps to the street.

'I love you too, Mummy.'

At least in the end, she and her parents had parted friends, Eleanor thought as she walked to the bus stop. It was one thing refusing to follow their carefully-laid plans, but quite another being on unfriendly terms — and despite assurances to herself that she felt otherwise, Eleanor was desperately sad not to have their blessing.

I'll make them proud of me.

At Paddington Station, Eleanor pushed through the crowded concourse to the platform and showed the ticket inspector her travel warrant. Many of her fellow passengers were in uniform — Army, Navy and Air Force, most with kitbags, tin hats, gas masks and rifles and she could hear accents from all around the British Isles as well as from further afield. Conversations between Canadians, Australians and South Africans mingled with languages she couldn't identify.

Eleanor found a third-class carriage and settled into a corner, after putting her suitcase on the luggage rack. Soon the carriage filled up with passengers including three WAAFs, a few Royal Navy ratings and some soldiers.

'Hello, darling!'

She looked up to see a tall, thin-faced girl who she recognised from school, although this young woman had been a year older than Eleanor.

'It is Eleanor, isn't it? Eleanor Taylor-Scott?'

Eleanor nodded, her cheeks burning as she noticed everyone in the carriage stare at her.

'I'm sure this lady will move up a bit for me to sit next to you.' She smiled at the woman sitting next to Eleanor. 'I'm only slim, so if you just move up a bit, I can . . . ' The girl squeezed in.

Eleanor was so squashed, she had almost turned sideways but the girl managed to cram in, taking no notice of the grumbling woman.

'You remember me, don't you?' the girl said loudly and Eleanor noticed one of the WAAF girls rolling her eyes to the ceiling.

'Connie Melford!' Eleanor said, pleased she'd suddenly remembered the girl's name.

'That's me!' Connie said loudly.

'Well, Connie,' one of the sailors said, 'p'raps you'd keep it down a bit. I'd like to get some kip. Some of us ain't just finished a game of hockey, some of us 'ave been on duty.'

Unabashed, Connie went on in a loud whisper.

'So, Eleanor, where are you off to?' But in what Eleanor soon found out was characteristic of Connie's questions, she didn't leave any time to answer. 'I've joined the WAAF!'

One WAAF girl groaned softly. Eleanor noticed another mouth *That's all we need* to her friend.

'Me too,' Eleanor said in a quieter whisper.

'Oh! How splendid! It's going to be such fun! Where are you off to?' And before Eleanor could reply, she went on, 'I'm going to RAF Abbsworth.'

'Me too,' Eleanor murmured, aware of the WAAFs exchanging dismayed glances. Finally, one of them couldn't remain quiet any longer.

'I hope you're not expecting it to be one long party, because it's jolly hard work.'

Unabashed, Connie said, 'Oh, we don't mind hard work, do we, Eleanor?

I muck out my own horses, you know.'

'Horses?' one of the WAAFs queried. 'You've got more than one?'

'Yes,' said Connie.

'Are you joining the mounted WAAF division?' one of the girls asked. Eleanor saw that for a second, her friends looked puzzled, before catching on to the joke.

'I didn't know there was one,' exclaimed Connie. 'Gosh, I'd be very interested. Daddy says I was born in the saddle. How do I find out about joining?'

'Just ask the Squadron Officer in Charge about the Pegasus Group.'

Connie was oblivious to the joke, even when the others burst out laughing.

Quietly, Eleanor said, 'Connie, they're pulling your leg.'

'Well, how unfriendly,' Connie said haughtily.

'You're not going to last long if you think the RAF use horses!' the WAAF said amid laughter.

After that, Connie kept quiet and shortly after, rocked by the rhythmic motion of the carriage and the warmth of bodies crushed together, she fell asleep, her head on Eleanor's shoulder.

It had never occurred to Eleanor that her upper-class accent set her apart from the very people she longed to fit in with. Connie obviously hadn't noticed the sideways glances and the eyes rolling as she spoke, and how the mention of 'Daddy' had set several of the girls giggling.

Connie, like Eleanor, came from a privileged background with plenty of money to cushion her from the unpleasant side of life. They'd gone to the same private girls' school, mixed in the same social circle and if the war hadn't started, would probably have married and later, attended bridge afternoons or cocktail parties at each other's houses. From their East London accents, the three WAAFs would probably have had a completely different upbringing.

Now, however, Eleanor desperately wanted to fit in. She wasn't going to be able to lose her accent but she would be careful of what words she used. Referring to her parents as Mummy and Daddy appeared likely to bring derision, and any mention of their wealth would be undesirable.

Eleanor's stomach growled with hunger. Her sandwiches were in her case on the luggage rack but she feared that if she moved, it might wake Connie and she'd disturb everyone again.

One of the WAAF girls smiled at her and held up a bag of sweets, as if offering her one. Eleanor smiled back and glanced at Connie, as if to say she dared not move. The girl nodded and leaned forward so that Eleanor only needed to raise her hand and select a sweet.

'Thank you,' she whispered.

'You're welcome,' the girl whispered back. Glancing at Connie, she gave Eleanor a sympathetic look. 'Not long now,' she added.

'Thank goodness for that,' the woman next to Connie said as the train pulled in and the WAAFs prepared to leave. She made a great show of moving into the corner Eleanor had vacated.

The girl who'd offered Eleanor a sweet waited for her on the platform. 'If you'd like to come with me, I'll show you where the transport lorry'll be. Get your papers ready. I'm Mary Ellis, by the way.'

'Connie Melford,' Connie said, taking the hand Mary was holding out to Eleanor.

'Eleanor Taylor.' Eleanor shook Mary's hand.

'Taylor-Scott,' corrected Connie.

'No,' said Eleanor, 'a double-barrelled name is just a mouthful. I want to be known as Taylor.'

'Please yourself,' said Connie. 'I'd never change my surname because it was a mouthful.'

Mary led them outside to a transport lorry and Eleanor handed her papers to the sergeant who indicated she should get into the back. Following the other girls' lead, Eleanor grabbed the rope hanging over the tailboard and hauled herself aboard, then sat on the bench next to Mary.

Connie decided it was too hard for her to climb aboard using the rope wearing her high-heeled shoes, so she asked the sergeant if she could ride in the front. The others giggled as the sergeant shouted. Connie suddenly appeared above the tailboard and flopped forward, half in and half out. The sergeant was obviously pushing and Connie fell in an undignified heap on the floor.

'How dare he!'

'Keep your voice down,' one of the other girls said, 'or you'll find yourself on jankers.'

'Jankers?' Connie said. 'I've no idea what that is but when I tell Daddy about his rough treatment, that sergeant won't know what hit him.'

'Oh dear,' whispered Mary to Eleanor while the other girls giggled.

'What's jankers?' Eleanor asked.

'Punishment. Mostly, it seems to come down to scrubbing floors. The worse the offence, the worse the floor you have to clean. The cookhouse is pretty bad but the ablutions . . . well.'

Eleanor had no idea what the ablutions were but was too embarrassed to show her ignorance again. Perhaps it would all become clear soon.

* * *

'I don't like travelling sideways,' Connie said, 'It makes me feel sick.'

'Don't worry,' Mary replied, checking her watch, 'only a few more minutes. Once we go round the sharp bend, we're nearly there.'

Seconds later, the lorry turned a corner and came to a halt.

'This can't be it,' said Connie, looking with dismay at the rows of grey Nissen huts linked by concrete paths. In the middle was a large square area on which several squads of girls were marching back and forth.

'Get used to it,' one of the WAAFs said. 'This is home sweet home until you get posted.'

'I can't stay here,' said Connie.

'Just give it a chance,' urged Eleanor. 'We haven't really seen any of it yet.'

Four other new girls had arrived in the lorry with Eleanor and Connie. They were taken first to the WAAF Squadron Officer in Charge who welcomed them and handed them over to a corporal who escorted them to one of the Nissen huts.

'I'm Corporal Jensen. This is Hut Three and I'm in charge. Any questions, come and ask me.'

About thirty beds were arranged along the two side walls. On each was piled three square pads. The corporal called them biscuits and showed them how to arrange them on the bed to make a mattress. A pillow, sheets and blankets were placed on the biscuits.

'It's cold in here,' said Connie. 'Why hasn't someone lit the fire?' She looked at the iron stove which appeared to be the only form of heating.

'Because the stove isn't lit before seventeen hundred hours,' Corporal Jensen replied. 'Now, if you'll follow me, I'll show you the ablutions.'

When Eleanor saw the hut containing the basins, baths and toilets with their concrete floor, she understood what Mary had meant when she said the worst type of jankers was scrubbing the ablutions' floor.

'It's so far away from where we sleep,' Connie said. 'I really don't think this is for us, Eleanor. I'm going to have a word with the Squadron Officer. This can't be right.'

'I'm fine, thanks,' Eleanor said brightly with a confidence she didn't feel. She definitely wasn't going to make a fuss and risk either getting into trouble or finding the other girls wouldn't accept her. Several of them had looked at Connie in irritation when she'd criticised some aspect of the camp.

Once they'd seen the ablutions, the

corporal said, 'Right, let's get you some irons and then you can get something to eat in the mess.' She pointed to a large hut at the end of the parade ground. 'After that, you'll go to the Medical department, over there.'

'Irons?' a shy-looking girl next to Eleanor asked.

'I don't know,' said Eleanor, 'but I have a feeling it'll be obvious, once we're given them.'

Irons turned out to be a knife, fork and spoon which were given to each girl, along with a large mug and a bag to keep them in.

'Bring your irons to every meal,' the corporal instructed, 'or you'll be eating with your fingers.'

Inside the mess, they were given stew, potatoes, swede and large chunks of bread, followed by apple crumble and tea.

The food wasn't very appetising but Eleanor was so hungry, she ate everything while the six girls chatted over their meal. Vera Martins, the shy girl, attached herself to Eleanor, telling her this was the first time she'd travelled away from Wales and her first time away from home.

Unusually, Connie was very quiet which gave everyone a chance to get to know each other.

When they'd finished, the corporal appeared and marched them to the Medical Officer.

'Time for your medicals, FFI and injections,' she said.

'What's FFI, Corporal?' one of the girls asked.

'Free From Infection.'

'What's that then, Corporal?'

'You'll soon find out.'

* * *

'Take my clothes off?' Connie shrieked. 'I most certainly will not. I demand to see the Squadron Officer.'

Eleanor stripped off with the other girls and closed her eyes as she was inspected for nits and other creatures.

Eventually the indignity was over and she was told to get dressed and be ready for injections. It had been hideously embarrassing but at least all the girls had gone through it together. One was kept back and Eleanor overheard the medical officer telling her she'd be fine after a haircut and paraffin treatment.

'Nits!' Vera said with revulsion. 'Oh, I couldn't bear to have nits!'

'Well, apparently you haven't,' said Eleanor, 'or you'd be in there with Enid, being treated.'

Corporal Jensen reappeared and led the group — minus Enid — to another hut which was full of counters covered in uniform and equipment.

'Give your measurements to the sergeant,' Corporal Jensen said and the girls marched forward to receive all the pieces which made up their uniform, including underwear.

'These are enormous!' Vera said, holding up one of the pairs of black, woollen knickers.

The girls struggled back to Hut Three

with a kitbag full of uniform, tin hats, gas masks, shoe brushes and a sewing kit.

It wasn't until they started to put their uniforms on that Eleanor realised Connie wasn't with them. Presumably she really had gone to see the Squadron Officer. Eleanor never found out because Connie didn't return.

* * *

'Ooh, you look so smart in your uniform, Ellie,' Vera said as she did up her shirt. 'You've got such a small waist. I look like a blue barrel.'

Vera had started to call Eleanor Ellie, and when they'd been joined by Lois, a cheeky Cockney, she'd assumed that was Eleanor's name.

Ellie Taylor. It sounded much less snooty than her real name and she accepted it gladly.

That first night at Abbsworth had been difficult for some of the girls, missing home and finding the lack of privacy and the hardship rather daunting. Ellie heard snuffles and snivels coming from under the blankets. She, too, was unsure of what the future held, although she'd telephoned her mother and told her everything was wonderful and that she'd met some new friends already.

The following morning at six o'clock, a klaxon sounded and Ellie got up quickly, realising there would be great demand for a sink in the ablution hut. If she didn't get in early, she might not get a wash at all. But soon, all the girls were putting on their new 'blues' and helping each other pin up long hair and tuck it into caps.

After breakfast, the girls spent the morning on the parade ground, marching back and forth, trying to keep in time with each other.

'Oh, Vera, that's yer left foot!' Lois whispered as Vera was told off again by Corporal Jensen. 'Come on, gal, or Jensen'll have us marching up and down all day!'

In the afternoon there was a demonstration on saluting, followed by a talk about the history of the Royal Air Force, and no more square-bashing until the following day.

As the weeks progressed, the girls spent more time on the parade ground until they could march like a single unit — and even Vera kept in time. They had psychological tests and learned more about the routine life of a WAAF. And they grew to enjoy each other's company.

Each morning, Ellie spent ages pinning up her plaits so that they wouldn't touch her collar — something which would have resulted in her being placed on a charge.

'I don't know why you don't let me cut it for you,' Vera said. 'I was a hairdresser back home.'

'Cut that lovely long 'air?' Lois said, aghast.

'Well, it's not as if it can be seen, is it?' Ellie countered. 'It's plaited and pinned up so tightly, I might be better off with it shorter.'

So, that evening after dinner, Vera placed a towel around Ellie's shoulders and snipped off the plaits. 'Righty-ho, well, there's no going back now,' she said cheerfully.

Holding the two plaits in her hands, Ellie wondered if she'd done the right thing.

'How long were you a hairdresser, Vera?'

'Well, the actual truth is, I wasn't ever a hairdresser as such.'

'What?'

'I was training, though. And I don't like to blow my own trumpet but I was rather good.'

Lois who was sitting on her bed watching, winced theatrically.

'Blimey, I ain't never seen such a pig's ear!'

Ellie squealed in alarm.

'I'm only joking, gal! Actually, it's looking good. P'raps you'll do mine when you've finished, Vera?'

Ellie peered into the mirror. Her hair

was very different — it fell in waves and appeared thicker. She looked older and more sophisticated.

Lois took the towel and sat waiting. Vera ran her fingers through her hair and keeping her normal voice, she winked at Ellie.

'I'm not sure there's anything I can do to this, it's like a thatched roof.'

' 'Ere! Don't be so cheeky!' Lois said.

At the end of their training period, they'd been transformed from a disorderly bunch of girls from a variety of backgrounds, with various levels of education, to a disciplined group of WAAFs who were well turned out and could march in time. They were called in one by one to the Squadron Officer to be told where they were to be posted.

'I hope we'll be together,' Vera said and the other two nodded.

'Well, it appears you've been put down to be a cook,' the Squadron Officer said to Ellie. 'Did you request that?'

'No — in fact I asked to do office work.'

'I see, well, I'll query it. And with your academic record, I believe you're officer material. I'll add that to your report too. Well, good luck at RAF Holsmere in Essex, Aircraft woman Second Class Taylor. And well done.'

The only thing to mar the passing-out parade was the knowledge that the three girls were being sent to the furthest reaches of the country.

'They couldn't 'ave put more distance between us if they'd tried,' wailed Lois who was headed up to Scotland, away from Vera on the south coast and Ellie in the east in Essex.

'I know,' said Vera sadly. 'It's like they did it on purpose.'

'Well, we'll all just have to put a lot of effort into writing to each other and keeping in touch. And you never know, one of us at least might get a posting somewhere different in the future.'

But the three girls were subdued as they tidied away their biscuits and bedding the following morning and ate their last breakfast together.

* * *

Ellie had one night's leave before she was due to join her new station and returned home with mixed feelings. Surely her parents would accept her decision to join up, once they saw how grownup she'd become?

Her mother held her hands to her mouth in horror when she saw Ellie's short hair.

'Oh, Eleanor! Did the RAF make you do that? Oh, how dreadful!'

Her father turned his head on one side, considered the new look carefully, then pronounced it was very modern and suited her.

'Well, you would know all about modern, wouldn't you, with all those young Wrens about!' her mother snapped.

Dinner was a strained affair and it was obvious to Ellie that her parents were now virtual strangers. From time to time, her mother couldn't resist voicing a sharp criticism of her father which he ignored — at least for the duration of her stay.

How strange it was to sleep in a proper bed once more without biscuits, which seemed to move apart as she slept. And how differently the staff behaved to her now that she was in uniform. She observed herself in the cheval mirror. There had been no full-length mirrors at Abbsworth but now, as she gazed at her reflection, she saw how different she was from the girl who'd once lived here. All her puppy fat had melted away and her face, once slightly round, had thinned, resulting in a pleasant heart shape. Her figure, too, was now shapely with the narrow waist that Vera had so admired and curvy bust and hips. She patted her hair into place. It might have shocked her mother but she liked the way her blonde waves arranged themselves artfully around her face.

In addition to all the things she could see in the mirror, there was something else. Something intangible. Was it the way she now stood? Upright, with her shoulders back as if she was glad to be alive? Or was it the way her eyes met her own, with confidence and determination?

'Eleanor!' her mother called up the stairs. 'Your cab will be here in a minute. Are you ready?'

Ellie saluted her reflection with a smile and, picking up her kitbag, she went down to the hall where her parents were waiting to say goodbye.

She asked the cab driver to let her out a short way from Liverpool Street Station and paid him with the money her father had pressed into her hand when she left. Other than Connie, who'd never turned up again at Abbsworth, all the WAAFs Ellie knew wouldn't have had money for a cab in London and would have arrived at the station by bus, on the Underground or on foot.

It might be different at Holsmere, but she didn't want to risk being singled out. Certainly not for things over which she had no control — like her parents' class or their wealth. The importance of first impressions had come home to her with force. It was one thing getting on with all the girls during her training, which had only lasted a few weeks, but quite another ensuring that she was fully accepted at her first posting.

Ellie wove her way through the crowds on the concourse, looking up at the numbers suspended over the ticket barrier entrance to each platform. Finally, she located hers and headed towards it, her travel warrant in her hand.

Near the barrier, a tall WAAF with auburn hair was kissing an RAF pilot passionately and Ellie wondered what would happen if a senior WAAF officer should see her. Certainly, all the officers she'd met so far would've put the girl on a charge, but perhaps they'd been particularly strict at Abbsworth. And after all, a war was on; life seemed to be more intense than before.

A voice came from next to Ellie.

'That's a disgrace to our uniform,' she said.

The girl was smaller than Ellie. She had an almost doll-like appearance with dark curls framing an oval face with skin which was perfect, just like china. She pushed her spectacles up her nose and turned her face as they passed the kissing couple.

'Are you going to Holsmere?' Ellie asked.

'Yes. It's my first posting. I've just finished training.'

'Me too,' said Ellie. 'I'm a bit nervous, so I'm pleased to have found someone in the same boat. I'm Ellie Taylor.'

'Jess Langley.'

The two girls found seats together in the third-class carriage and settled down for the journey. Seconds before the whistle blew, the girl who'd been kissing the pilot entered the carriage.

'Ah,' she said when she saw Ellie and Jess, 'I thought I saw two WAAFs get on the train. I don't suppose you're going to Holsmere, are you?'

'I don't know how you saw anything,'

Jess said disdainfully. 'You looked quite engrossed to me.'

'It always pays to keep your eyes peeled, whatever you're doing,' said the new girl. 'I'm Kitty, by the way, Kitty Spencer.'

The other two girls introduced themselves and Kitty sat opposite them.

'This is my first posting,' she said and for a second, Ellie detected an anxious look in Kitty's eyes, despite her apparent confidence.

'It's our first posting too,' Ellie said. 'Where's your sweetheart stationed?'

Kitty laughed.

'Sweetheart? Oh no, he's not my sweetheart!'

'Are you married?' Jess looked relieved.

'Good gracious, no! Bill's devilishly handsome but he's rather dull.'

'Why were you kissing him so passionately, then?' Jess asked.

'Why not? It was just a bit of fun.'

'Men get the wrong idea if you act like that.'

'He's already got the wrong idea. But I put him straight. There's no way I'm getting married yet,' Kitty said with a laugh.

'What! He's asked you to marry him?'

'Oh, yes.'

'You're lucky no officers saw you and put you on a charge,' said Jess darkly.

'Born lucky, I suppose,' Kitty said but her earlier carefree attitude had changed and she spoke with a bitter edge to her voice. 'Well, now you've made it clear you disapprove of my behaviour, I'll have to pull my socks up if we're going to be friends. So, tell me about yourselves.'

Jess's family lived in an ancient, crumbling vicarage in a small village in Kent, where her father was vicar and her mother tried to keep on top of the mice in their home and in the thirteenth-century church. Her elder brother had joined the army as soon as he was of age, so she spent most of her time reading and doing puzzles.

Ellie said she lived in London with her parents, giving the impression her mother was a housewife and her father a lowly rank in the Royal Navy.

Kitty, Ellie realised later, had given away little about her family but spent the journey making them laugh with stories from her WAAF training.

By the time they alighted at the station, Ellie felt she'd known the two girls for some time, probably because Kitty was such good company. Even Jess appeared to be won over.

A sergeant directed them to the transport and they climbed aboard using the rope at the end of the lorry, to sit on the benches amongst other WAAFs and airmen, all bound for Holsmere.

The Squadron Officer in charge of the WAAFs greeted the new recruits at the station and left it to the duty sergeant to show them around and tell them where they were to be billeted.

'Let's see if we can stick together, shall we, Ellie?' said Kitty.

The duty sergeant took the six new WAAF girls around the station, showing them the Officers' Mess, their mess, the canteen, the Operations Room and the NAAFI, where they could buy items such as stationery, stamps and toiletries, as well as snacks. The sight of the aircraft hangars and the Vickers Wellington bombers lined up — some with ground crew working on them — was a sobering reminder of exactly why they were all there, deep in the Essex countryside.

'I need two volunteers to billet in a room in Hillside Cottage,' the duty sergeant said and as Kitty was about to raise her hand, Ellie stopped her. 'What about Jess?' she said.

Two girls stepped forward and took the sheet of paper with the details of how to find Hillside Cottage.

'The rest of you will be billeted at Larkrise Farm,' he said, handing Ellie the details.

As well as Ellie, Jess and Kitty, there was one other girl. She had an exotic look with golden brown skin and glossy, dark hair cut in a bob.

'Hello,' she said, holding out her hand. 'I'm Genevieve Lawrence. I can see you're good friends already, I hope I won't get in the way.'

'Oh, no!' said Jess. 'We've only just met but I have a feeling we're all going to get along.'

* * *

A warm welcome awaited the girls at Larkrise Farm. Mr and Mrs Ringwood showed them around their sprawling farmhouse and explained they were out most of the day, during which time the girls could use the kitchen but since the farm's rations wouldn't feed them all, they requested that the girls ate in their canteen at the station.

Jess seemed quite pleased when Kitty assumed she and Ellie would share one bedroom and Jess and Genevieve would share the other.

'I don't think Jess approves of me,'

Kitty said when she and Ellie were alone. 'Oh, I don't mind,' she added, when Ellie said she was sure that wasn't the case.

Their rooms were basic but at least they had beds and warm, crocheted blankets.

'Much better than those dreadful biscuits,' Kitty said with a laugh. 'Who in their right mind would design a mattress in three pieces?'

That evening, the four girls walked back to the station for dinner, carrying their irons. They would all have one night's sleep and then the following day would be told when their shifts began.

Kitty was a driver, Jess a wireless operator and Genevieve a plotter.

'Cook?' said Kitty, when Ellie told them what her trade was. 'I'd never have thought that.'

'Me neither. I requested office work.'

'Oh, the vagaries of RAF logic,' Kitty said. 'Oh well, I'm sure you can re-muster.'

'What does that mean?' Genevieve asked.

'Change trades,' said Kitty. 'Only you'd better not do it immediately, they might send you away to train elsewhere and we've only just moved in together. I don't want a new roommate so soon!'

They queued with their plates. One WAAF dolloped mashed potato on each plate, another cabbage and a third, mince. Further along the line, apple tart and custard were served.

As Ellie ate, she watched the WAAFs working in the canteen, knowing the following morning, she'd be joining them. The corporal in charge was a large, pot-bellied man with a red face, whose voice could often be heard above the hubbub of the air and ground crew eating at the long tables and benches in the Nissen hut canteen.

Well, it doesn't look too difficult, Ellie thought, *just hard work. And it's vital work because everyone needs to be fed*.

'I bet that corporal's all right when you get to know him,' Kitty said with a sympathetic smile.

While they ate, they asked Genevieve about her life. She was half-French, her mother having come to England from Marseilles to learn the language in her early twenties. She'd met Genevieve's father and never gone home.

'You must get your exotic looks from your mother,' Kitty said. 'I love your hair, it's so silky.'

'What shall we do now?' Kitty asked as they came out of the canteen.

'Let's go back to the billet,' Jess said. 'It's nearly dark now and we've got to be up early. Don't forget we've got a walk to the station in the morning. It's not like when we were training and we fell out of our huts on to the parade ground.'

'I'm with Jess,' said Genevieve. 'I'm really tired. I'm going back to a cup of cocoa and bed.'

'Ellie?' Kitty asked.

Ellie really wanted to go to bed too, but didn't want to disappoint her new roommate.

'What did you have in mind?'

'Let's ask someone where the nearest pub is.' She strode off before anyone could reply.

'Well, Genevieve? I can almost smell the cocoa,' Jess said, throwing Ellie a sympathetic glance before setting off to Larkrise Farm.

Ellie expected Kitty to go back into the canteen to find one of the WAAFs to ask but to her surprise, she headed towards the Officers' Mess.

'Kitty? Where are you going?'

If Kitty heard, she didn't reply.

'Kitty! You can't go in there! It's for officers only. You'll be doing jankers before you've even started work!'

'I'm not going in,' Kitty said, 'but no one can get in or out without us seeing, and I'll just stop someone when they pass us.'

'We could go back to the canteen or in the NAAFI and find a WAAF to ask,' suggested Ellie.

'Who wants to go to the pub with a group of WAAFs? And if we're lucky — '

Ellie never heard what Kitty hoped

might happen if they were lucky because the door opened and a pilot came out, closely followed by another.

'Good evening, sir,' Kitty said politely to the first man, as she saluted. 'I wonder if you could direct my friend and myself to the nearest pub. We arrived today and haven't had time to explore.'

By the light of the full moon, Ellie saw that the first pilot had fair hair and the second was dark. From the insignia on their sleeves, she could just make out they were both Flight Lieutenants.

'What luck, eh, Sonny?' the fair-haired pilot said to his friend. 'We're just off for a pint ourselves. Perhaps you ladies would join us?'

Kitty grabbed Ellie's arm and pulled her after the two pilot officers.

Ellie was glad of the darkness to hide her blushes. Kitty had been so obvious and although the first pilot seemed happy for them to accompany him, the other remained silent.

Kitty let go of her friend's arm and

walked alongside the fair-haired pilot who introduced himself as Leo. 'Flight Lieutenant Vincent, if we're on duty,' he added, 'and this is Flight Lieutenant Rayment. Or Sonny to his friends.'

'I'm Aircraftwoman Second Class Spencer, or Kitty. Ellie is Aircraftwoman Second Class Taylor.'

'I hope you're not related to Air Marshal Spencer, or Sonny and I'll have to mind our Ps and Qs!'

'No,' said Kitty quickly, 'it's a common name.'

Leo led them to a car. 'My MG PB Four-Seater Sports Tourer,' he said proudly, taking the cover off the seats in the back. 'Hop in.'

Ellie got in the back, expecting Kitty to follow but she made it clear she intended to sit in the front passenger seat next to Leo, so Sonny climbed into the back.

'Hold tight!' Leo yelled as he reversed and swung the car round to head for the gate.

Kitty whooped with joy and waved

her cap as they drove down the road, past the turn-off for Larkrise Farm, where Ellie imagined Jess and Genevieve sipping cocoa or even tucked up in bed. She wished she'd gone with them. Sonny obviously hadn't welcomed their intrusion and Leo and Kitty were flirting so outrageously, Ellie was embarrassed. Well, let it be a lesson to her!

The village was about half a mile past the turn-off for the farm. Ellie knew she'd easily be able to walk home from the pub — it was a straight road. Of course, in the dark, she'd have to make sure she didn't walk straight past the narrow turn-off for the farm but even if she did, she'd merely end up at the station and have to turn around.

She'd have one drink, claim exhaustion and leave. Kitty wouldn't even notice. And if she was with Leo, surely he'd drop her home on his way back to the station. He was an officer, after all.

'The Wild Boar,' Leo announced as he pulled up outside the pub on the village green.

'Well, I hope there aren't any.' Kitty laughed.

'What?'

'Wild boar, of course!'

'No,' said Leo, 'although we seem to have an old bore with us!' He nudged Sonny. 'Come on, old man! It doesn't do to dwell on things . . . '

Sonny nodded. Forgetting Kitty for a moment, Leo draped his arm around his friend's shoulders and led them all into the pub.

'Evening, Tom,' Leo called to the landlord. 'Two pints of your special and whatever the ladies want.'

'Comin' up, sir!' Tom laid down his teacloth and took two tankards from the shelf. 'Ladies?'

'Scotch for me, please,' Kitty called.

Ellie, unused to drinking and with no idea what to order, said, 'Same for me, please.'

They sat at a table for four but it soon became obvious that Kitty and Leo were wrapped up in each other. Sonny leaned back, holding his pint and Ellie sipped her drink. It was revolting but she didn't feel she could simply announce she was going home without having drunk it. Taking a larger sip, she choked as the fiery liquid burned the back of her throat, making her eyes water.

'Sorry,' she said feeling foolish, 'it went down the wrong way.' But Kitty and Leo hadn't even noticed she'd choked.

Sonny leaned forward with a smile.

'All right now?' he asked kindly.

How stupid and childish he must think her. He obviously hadn't wanted female company; if he had, he could've had the pick of the station. He was so handsome and had such beautiful eyes, she thought — although they seemed very sad.

She dared not stare at him but his eyes kept drawing hers. As he glanced across the bar at a group of airmen who'd just entered, she let her gaze rest on his face. It seemed familiar, but she was certain she'd never met anyone called Sonny Rayment before. Nevertheless, there was something about him that was so familiar.

He turned back to her and caught her staring.

'Excuse me, I've just seen some of the ground crew who've been working on P for Pip. I'm just going to check how they've got on.'

Ellie knew each aircraft was given a letter, to which was added the RAF spelling alphabet word to help avoid confusion over the radio — A for Apple, B for Beer and so on. So, Sonny's aircraft had the letter P, to which was added Pip.

He got up and after touching Leo's shoulder lightly he tipped his head towards the new arrivals. Leo nodded briefly and gave Sonny a sympathetic look, then turned back to Kitty.

This is my chance. Ellie gulped the rest of the Scotch, screwed up her face with the effort of swallowing it without choking, and rose.

'I'm exhausted,' she said to Kitty. 'I

hope you won't mind if I leave you.'

'But how will you get back?' Kitty asked.

'I'll walk. Don't worry, it's just a straight road.'

'Well, if you're sure . . .'

It was obvious Kitty didn't want to leave.

'Yes, it's a lovely moonlit night.'

'I can drive you home, if you like,' Leo offered.

'I wouldn't hear of it, thanks.' Ellie felt guilty at leaving Kitty, but unwilling to interrupt further.

'I'll be as quiet as a mouse when I get back,' Kitty promised. Ellie doubted that. Already on her second Scotch, Kitty's laugh was getting louder.

Ellie stood up, holding on to the back of her chair. She hadn't expected the alcohol to affect her so quickly but her head was spinning and her legs felt unsteady. Slipping her coat on, she concentrated on walking to the door without staggering or tripping.

The air was cold and her breath

billowed around her, but the chill cut through the haze that had taken over her brain. Doing up the buttons of her coat, she walked away from the pub with relief.

Having made his excuses to talk to his ground crew, Sonny wouldn't have returned to their table and Leo and Kitty were only interested in each other. By the time she arrived home, hopefully, the cold night air would have sobered her completely.

Inside the Wild Boar, someone started to play a piano and male voices joined it, singing a song she didn't recognise. The sound grew louder as someone opened the door and either entered or left, then faded as the door closed once more.

'Ellie!' a man called.

It was Sonny. Ellie's heart sank.

'Are you walking home?' he asked.

'Yes.'

'D'you mind if I walk with you?'

'No, but I'm perfectly all right on my own, if you'd rather not.'

'No, I'd like some company but Leo's too busy at the moment with your friend.'

'He seems quite taken with Kitty.'

'A word of warning,' Sonny said with a laugh. 'Leo is taken with pretty much any woman he meets, if they show the slightest interest in him. And your friend seems very interested.'

'Well, I only met Kitty this morning, but I'd say she's a match for your Leo, any day. From things she's said and from when I first laid eyes on her, she's quite taken with any man who shows interest in her and even those who don't! So they might be good for each other!'

'What was she doing when you first saw her?'

'Probably best I don't tell! How long have you been at Holsmere?' she asked, to divert him from Kitty's shortcomings. He was, after all, an officer.

'A few months. I joined up before war was declared and for a time, I trained new pilots but I wanted to see action. I . . . I . . . ' He paused. 'Well, I just wanted to do my bit. So, now I fly a Wellington Bomber.'

'P for Pip?'

He laughed. 'You were paying attention! Let me guess, you're a wireless operator?'

'No.'

'A plotter?'

'No. I wanted to work in administration but for some reason I was put in the canteen as a cook.'

'That's the RAF for you. But there's nothing wrong with that,' he added.

'No, but I wanted to feel I was really contributing to the war effort.'

'Food's probably the most important thing on an RAF station!'

'I suppose so. But it's not like being a pilot. You must feel like you're making a huge difference.'

Sonny was silent for a moment, then sighed.

'There's a price to be paid though,' he said, his voice suddenly serious and sad. 'Our last mission was to destroy an ammunition factory near Düsseldorf but P for Pip was hit by flak. We were badly shot up. That's why I just went to check with the ground crew if she was operational. Thankfully, the lads have got her going.' He paused. 'But Wainwright, my rear gunner, was shot. We put a tourniquet on his arm and he was alive when I landed but . . . I heard just before we came out that he didn't make it. He died in hospital. He was eighteen. He'd been with us three weeks.'

'Oh, Sonny, I'm so sorry! That's awful. How can you bear it?'

'The truth is . . . I can't. But you have to carry on anyway.'

'I'm so sorry.' No wonder Sonny had seemed distracted when Ellie had first met him.

They walked in silence for a while and then Sonny stopped. 'Can you hear the barn owl?'

'Yes! How wonderful! I didn't know that's what it was. It's not something you often hear in the middle of London.'

'Is that where you used to live?'

'Yes. I'm used to traffic, horses clip-clopping and voices, so it's going to take time to get used to the sounds of the country. At Abbsworth, we didn't go out at night. All I heard was the other girls snoring. But here, the night's full of sound.'

As if on cue, a startlingly loud screech came from the woods at the side of the road.

'What on earth's that?' Ellie jumped.

'Just a fox calling its mate.' He laughed. 'Don't worry, it sounds more frightening than it is.'

'You obviously come from the country,' she said.

Sonny didn't reply. He stopped and held his arm out to prevent her moving forward.

'Look!' he said, 'Over there!'

It took several seconds before she saw what he was pointing at. Two small, bright lights were glowing in the dark undergrowth and as Ellie watched, motionless and silent, a sleek shadow emerged into the moonlight. The fox sniffed the air, then scurried across the road ahead of them. As it gazed at them, its eyes reflected the silver light of the moon, making them appear like lamps. Then it slipped into the bushes and was gone.

'Oh, how wonderful!' Ellie whispered. 'I've only seen a fox in the zoo before.'

Sonny started to walk again.

'I often go into the woods to watch the wildlife when I'm not on duty. I can unwind and forget there's a war on for a short while. Perhaps one day, when you've settled in, of course, and you've got some time off, you'd like to come with me.'

'Oh, I'd love to!'

'I've got an op tomorrow night, but perhaps after that?'

She noticed he placed his palm against his chest and as he caught her gaze, he smiled.

'It's just my lucky ritual. All the pilots have one, or a lucky charm which they always take on their ops. It's all superstition but I don't know anyone who doesn't have something to bring them luck. Mine's a locket my mother gave me.'

He hooked his finger under the chain around his neck and allowed the heart-shaped locket to slip out of his collar, spinning in the moonlight.

'It's got a photograph of my parents in one side and my sisters in the other.' He tucked it back inside his collar. 'Leo has a lucky ring he wears on his right hand, and as he gets in G for George — his Wimpy — he touches it to the fuselage.'

'Wimpy?'

'Pet name for the Wellington Bomber. It's almost like they're part of the family too. I expect you think that's all nonsense.'

'Oh, not at all! I think you're all so very brave. It must be awful to know you're risking your lives each time you fly.'

'You get used to it,' he said, but she

had the feeling that wasn't true.

'How many ops have you flown?' she asked.

'Twenty-seven. This is my first operational tour and if I make it to thirty, I'll get some time off away from the station. A few pilots don't start a second operational tour once they've completed one — they become instructors or do other vital work. But if I'm lucky enough to survive — ' he placed his hand on his chest again — 'I'll definitely do a second tour. A third if necessary. I'll keep going as long as it takes. Sorry,' he said, his tones softening, 'that probably sounded a bit harsh.'

'Not at all,' she said, startled by his passion. But what did she know of soaring above the clouds over Germany, expecting a fighter aircraft to swoop from nowhere at any moment and shoot at you? Especially when you saw good men die, just as Sonny had with the young rear gunner.

'What's that?' Ellie asked in alarm as something in the woods grunted and rustled the undergrowth. It sounded like a large animal.

'It might be a badger. Or a wild boar. Or even an old bore.'

She looked at him quickly, recognising that Leo had referred to him as an old bore earlier and wondered if he was angry, but he was smiling.

'It's all right. Pilots pull each other's legs unmercifully. It's one of the ways we cope. If you didn't find the humour in something, you'd just . . . '

Even though she didn't really understand what it was like to be a pilot, Ellie wanted him to know she cared. For a second, she thought of just slipping her hand in his but she was afraid he'd assume she was like Kitty.

'Here's where you turn off,' he said.

'Well, thank you for walking me home. I'd have been frightened on my own — especially when that badger, or whatever it was, ran past.'

'I'm not leaving you here,' he said. 'I'll walk you to the door.'

'Oh, no! It's out of your way. I

couldn't ask you to do that.'

'You didn't ask me — I offered. The path's rutted and the hedge is throwing it in shadow. And of course, you have to be careful of wild boar . . .' He smiled, took her arm and they picked their way through the ruts to the farmhouse.

'There's a dance in the NAAFI on Saturday,' he said.

She waited, her heart pounding.

'And I was wondering . . . well, I was wondering if you'd like to go with me?' he asked.

'Oh, yes,' she said. 'Yes please, that would be lovely.'

As he turned to walk away, she called, 'Would a WAAF be allowed to wish a pilot luck for his next op? Or would that be considered unlucky?'

'Well, it's fine by me,' he said.

'Good luck for tomorrow night,' she said, placing her hand on her chest at the same time as he did the same.

'Good night, Ellie,' he said with a smile when he saw her gesture.

* * *

Genevieve and Jess had gone to bed when Ellie let herself into the kitchen. If they'd had cocoa, they'd cleaned the mugs and put them away. Or perhaps they'd gone straight to bed.

The horrible spinning in her head from the Scotch had gone, but it had been replaced by a very giddy feeling which seemed to get worse every time she remembered anything Sonny had said on their walk home. She recalled his laugh and the touching way he'd placed his hand on the outside of his shirt, covering the heart-shaped locket his mother had given him. He'd been nothing like she'd imagined when she first met him — morose and distant. But then, he'd obviously jumped to conclusions about her, since she was friends with Kitty.

A shiver of fear ran through her. Tomorrow night, he'd take off in one of those enormous Wellingtons with his crew, flying among German fighter planes intent on shooting them down, and over searchlights which would illuminate them so the anti-aircraft guns could take aim.

She crept up the rickety stairs, trying not to wake the two other girls and after undressing in the cold and dark, she slipped into bed.

The next thing she knew, her alarm clock was ringing. She sat up, wondering where Kitty was, but to her relief, she saw her roommate in the other bed stretch and yawn. Against all odds, Kitty had come in without making a noise. Or perhaps Ellie had just been so tired, she hadn't heard her.

'Morning, Ellie,' Kitty said. 'What a glorious night I had! Leo is simply divine. And so handsome! He's asked me to the dance at the NAAFI on Saturday. I'll tell the others about it at breakfast. Please say you'll come, too.'

'Yes.' Ellie's cheeks reddened. For some reason she didn't want to tell Kitty about Sonny asking her. For Kitty, life seemed to be a game. And last night, Ellie felt she and Sonny hadn't been simply playing games. But perhaps she was wrong. After all, she had no experience of men.

Genevieve and Jess had slept well and once they were all ready, they made their way to the station canteen for breakfast.

'This'll be the last time I have breakfast with you all,' Ellie said, eyeing the girl serving porridge. 'I'll be making it from tomorrow.'

'Well, perhaps you'll do something about the colour of the porridge tomorrow,' Genevieve said. 'Is it supposed to be grey?'

'It'll fill a hole,' said Kitty cheerily. 'You'll be glad of it in a few hours.'

'Filling holes is about all it's good for,' said Genevieve. 'It has the colour of cement.'

Ellie anxiously watched the girls serving. One was perspiring so hard, beads of sweat were standing out on her brow. Every so often, she could hear the corporal in charge of the cookhouse raise his voice as he hurried the WAAFs along.

Would it be like that all day? she wondered.

When she reported for duty, Corporal Noones, the man she'd heard shouting at breakfast, barely greeted her, simply pointing to the floor.

'Mop that up. I won't have a messy floor in my kitchen. Any time you see anything spilt, clear it up or someone'll break their neck.' He paused, hands on hips. 'Well, what're you waiting for, Taylor? A written invitation?'

'No, Corporal, it's just I don't know where the mops and buckets are kept.'

'Honestly,' he said, shaking his head. 'When you've got a dog, you don't expect to bark yerself! Over 'ere!'

He led Ellie to the cupboard. Still shaking his head, he walked off to shout at another girl.

One of the WAAFs who was peeling a great mound of potatoes and tossing them in an enormous pot smiled sympathetically.

'Is bark's worse than 'is bite,' she said. ''e lays it on a bit thick when new girls start, so they don't give 'im no trouble. When you've cleaned up, come an' 'elp me. Corp likes it when we show initiative. I'm Doreen, by the way. That's Norah over there and Marge spreading the marge on all those slices of bread. Corp thinks it's funny to have Marge on the marge. He's a funny little man but 'e's decent when you get to know 'im.'

Ellie mopped up and took out the rubbish, which won her a grateful glance from Corporal Noones, although he didn't say anything. Then she helped Doreen peel potatoes.

'We get through mounds of these, as I expect you can imagine,' she said. 'Mashin' 'em's a bit of a problem but Norah always helps. She's got muscles on her muscles.'

Doreen chuckled and Ellie looked at Norah, who was chopping cabbage. She did, indeed, look stocky and strong, with bulging biceps.

Ellie worked hard, helping where she could. From time to time, she caught Corporal Noones looking at her with something like approval.

As it got closer to lunchtime, the pace began to accelerate. Corporal Noones filled a plate with chops, mashed potato, cabbage and carrots, then placed a cover over the top. Taking a bowl, he filled it with suet pudding and custard, then covering that, he put the plate and bowl on a tray.

Ellie wondered why the other girls turned away, appearing to be extra busy at the sight of the tray.

'You, Taylor!' Corporal Noones said. 'Take this to Group Captain Hollingsworth's office.'

Ellie picked up the tray.

'Don't dawdle! It'll be cold when you get there!'

Ellie set off as fast as she dared and felt that now the tray had gone, the girls in the cookhouse had become more relaxed. Perhaps Group Captain Hollingsworth was hard to please.

'Go through,' the WAAF who was obviously the Group Captain's secretary said and Ellie knocked gingerly on the door.

'Come in.'

Ellie entered, 'Your lunch, sir.'

A gaunt man sat behind his desk, with piles of paper in front of him.

'What? Oh, yes, put it down over there.' He waved his hand vaguely at a table by the window. Ellie moved a few items and laid the tray down. She didn't know whether she ought to leave the covers or take them with her and she hovered uncertainly. Suddenly, the man groaned and clutched the arms of his chair. 'What are you waiting for?' he shouted. 'Get out!'

Ellie fled.

'Cecily!' he called and the secretary rushed into his office, slamming the door.

'How was Hollingsworth?' Doreen asked. 'The last time I took a meal, 'e told me I'd taken too much. But the corp puts the meal out. When I told the corp what Hollingsworth 'ad said, 'e just ignored me and put out as much the next time.'

'He didn't get as far as looking at how much food there was. He just told me to get out.'

'Well, to be fair,' said Doreen, ''e's got an 'eavy weight on 'is shoulders. I wouldn't want to send young men off over Germany to their almost certain deaths.'

When Ellie went back to pick up the tray, she was grateful to find Group Captain Hollingsworth wasn't in his office. From the marks on the plates, it looked as though the food had been scraped off, rather than eaten. Perhaps by the time he'd got to the meal, it was cold. Although with the war on, wasting food was quite unacceptable.

The following day when Ellie took the group captain his lunch, he was on the telephone and he waved at her to leave it on the table, which she did and escaped quickly. When she got back, Norah had spilled custard on the floor and Corporal Noones was shouting at her for wasting food and making a mess, so Ellie helped clear up and then put margarine on piles of bread slices.

'Go and pick up the Group Captain's tray, Taylor,' Corporal Noones said.

'Yes, Corp,' Ellie said, hoping he would be occupied on the telephone or even better, out of the office when she got there.

When she arrived, Cecily, the secretary wasn't there and the door was ajar, so she tapped gently, assuming Group Captain Hollingsworth wasn't inside. She entered, not seeing anyone, but at the sound of her footsteps the senior officer, who'd been leaning over behind his desk, sat up.

'Oh, I'm sorry, sir!' Ellie felt the blood drain from her face with shock.

Instead of shouting at her, as she'd expected, his sunken cheeks reddened, as if he'd been caught out. A cat walked around the desk towards her, a chunk of meat held daintily in its jaws. It looked up at her as if surprised that she should be in its way, then walked towards the corner.

'Ah,' said Group Captain Hollingsworth, as if his actions needed some explanation. Then he bent over again and picked up the plate which had been on the floor.

'Err . . . what's your name?' he asked.

'Taylor, sir.'

'Your first name.'

'Ellie, sir.'

'Well, Ellie, I expect you're wondering what's going on.'

'Oh, no, sir. Well, yes, sir, but I'm sure it's none of my business, sir.'

'A good answer, Ellie. Since you've been honest, I will be too. I've lost my appetite a bit lately and it doesn't matter how often I ask for my meals to be reduced in size, they come up just as big. So I thought Socrates might help me out. Now, I'm sure you know that would be frowned upon — feeding a cat with food for a human during wartime isn't the done thing. But I simply can't bear to look at the food at the moment.'

'I'm so sorry, sir.'

'I wasn't asking for your pity, Ellie.'

'No, sir, of course not.'

'So, if you come tomorrow, please could you bring me smaller portions. I'm sure someone else would be grateful for extra rations. You're welcome to it yourself.'

'Oh, no, sir, I couldn't do that. But the problem is that Corporal Noones always serves your food. Doreen told me she'd passed on your request but he didn't seem to take any notice.'

'Leave it to me, Ellie. I didn't realise . . . Oh, and yesterday, when I shouted at you. Well, I apologise.'

'That's perfectly fine, sir.'

'I know this is a strange thing to ask, Ellie and I am asking you — not ordering you — if you can keep what you saw with Socrates to yourself.'

'Yes, sir, of course, sir.'

'Good. Thank you.'

* * *

The following day, Corporal Noones told Ellie to prepare the tray for Group Captain Hollingsworth and take it across to his office, on the double.

'Yes, corp,' Ellie said.

She placed a small amount of each item on the plate and a spoonful of pudding with a tiny amount of custard, then covered the plates and set off for the group captain's office.

'Thank you, Ellie,' he said, seeing the greatly reduced amounts of food. 'I just can't face a whole plateful. This is much more what I need.'

As she was about to leave, his telephone rang. Seconds later, Cecily's telephone started to ring.

Ellie had seen the secretary with a pile of papers walking towards the Officers' Mess on her way in, so she knew Cecily wasn't there.

'Shall I answer it?' she asked, pointing to Cecily's telephone.

The Group Captain nodded and smiled.

'Good afternoon, Group Captain

Hollingsworth's office,' Ellie said in her clearest voice and carefully noted down the message.

Ellie knew she'd get into trouble with Corporal Noones when she got back to the canteen for taking so long but she could tell from the nature of the message she'd taken that Group Captain Hollingsworth was in the middle of a crisis and she thought she'd take her chance.

By the time Cecily returned, Ellie had taken several messages and was looking for a file in one of the secretary's drawers. When she saw Cecily, she jumped back, not sure if the older woman would approve of her searching through her files, but she needn't have worried. Cecily was glad of the help and grateful Ellie had assisted the group captain, for whom she seemed to have a great deal of affection.

'It's a shame you didn't choose clerical work,' Cecily said. 'You're a natural and I can see the group captain likes you. I'm going to be leaving soon — ' she patted her stomach —

'I've got a little one on the way. I'd be much happier knowing the group captain had a secretary he liked.'

'I did choose clerical work,' Ellie said, 'but for some reason, I was put into the cookhouse.'

'Leave it with me,' said Cecily. 'If you'd like, of course.'

'Oh yes!'

Cecily accompanied Ellie back to the canteen with the tray and had a word with Corporal Noones who glowered at Ellie but didn't say any more.

* * *

By the day of the dance, Ellie knew Sonny had flown on two successful missions to the Ruhr. He had one more and then he'd be given leave. She too, would be away, training. She would learn shorthand, typing and other office skills which would get her out of the canteen. Doreen, Norah and Marge said they were sorry to see her go so quickly. Even Corporal Noones wished her well.

'Blimey, 'e must like yer!' Doreen said. ''E gave a right earful to the last girl who left!'

Ellie was excited. Finally, she'd be training to work in an office — and that evening, she'd be meeting Sonny in the NAAFI for the dance.

On the nights Sonny had been flying, Ellie had gone to the ops room ostensibly to wait for Genevieve, but actually to check that P for Pip had returned safely. She hadn't said she had a date — Genevieve and Jess were both scandalised by Kitty's behaviour with men, and Ellie didn't want them to assume she was like her. But at the dance, what would be more natural than that she should meet someone? And that someone would be Flight Lieutenant Sonny Rayment.

'Well, at least the NAAFI's been decorated,' Kitty said. 'I've never been to a dance in a blue uniform before. I can't believe we're not allowed to dress up.'

'Oh, honestly, Kitty, there is a war

on, you know!' Jess said. 'And none of us have dresses.'

'There are always ways and means,' Kitty said with a laugh.

'Someone's taken a lot of effort with the NAAFI,' Genevieve said. 'So much coloured paper and balloons! It looks quite pretty!'

'Just like us!' said Kitty. 'Even with our uniforms!'

'Is that Leo?' Ellie asked, pointing to where a group of airmen were setting up their instruments.

'Yes,' said Kitty. 'He's singing with the band. Hopefully not all evening — I want a dance.'

Leo had a wonderful voice and sang the first few numbers before leaving the band members and joining Kitty. Sonny had already found Ellie and they danced together.

'I'm sorry,' he said, 'I'm afraid I'm not very good at dancing. But you're wonderful.'

She didn't mention that her mother had paid for special dancing lessons so she could impress prospective suitors. All that seemed so far away.

Halfway through the evening, Sonny suggested they go outside for some fresh air. The NAAFI was thick with cigarette smoke and Ellie's eyes were stinging. It was cold but still, and Sonny put his arm around her to keep her warm. How wonderful it was to be so close to him.

'I've one more op,' he said, briefly holding his hand to his chest, 'then I've got some time off. I don't suppose you could get a few days off?'

Her heart raced. She hadn't expected him to want to spend his well-earned rest with her. But it was impossible; she'd be leaving the station for several weeks to carry out her training. She told him her good news.

'That's marvellous,' he said. 'I'm so glad you're going to do what you really wanted to do. And at least, when I come back, you'll be here.'

'Are you definitely coming back?'

'I hope so. That's the plan, anyway.

And if you're going to be here . . . I hope you don't mind, Ellie, but ever since we walked home from the pub the other night, I can't get you off my mind.'

'I . . . I felt the same,' she said, 'but we don't really know each other . . . '

'Then we need to put that right. Starting now! So, tell me your favourite colour, your favourite food, your pet hates, your — '

'Stop, I can't keep up!' she said, 'Now, let me see . . . I like the colour blue, and chocolate. I don't like rats, being cold, peeling potatoes . . . How about you?'

He caught hold of her hand. 'Blue, rats, being cold, peeling potatoes — just like you. See! We're a perfect match.'

'Your pet hate's peeling potatoes? You just made that up. I bet you've never peeled a potato in your life!'

'Oh, how little you know about me!'

'Well, tell me more!' she said.

'How about I show you?'

He placed his hands behind her shoulders and drew her towards him, his eyes questioning hers. In response, she put her arms around his neck and allowed him to kiss her gently on the lips.

When he broke away, she gasped with surprise. A few boys had stolen kisses from her at the various social gatherings she'd been to but they had been awkward, embarrassing incidents which hadn't been enjoyable in the slightest.

But Sonny's kiss! It had started a cascade of sensations which rippled through her body.

'Was that a gasp of pleasure or horror?' he asked.

'Oh, definitely pleasure, Flight Lieutenant Rayment. In fact, I may have to add it to my list of favourite things.'

'I was very much hoping it might become top of the list of all your favourite things!'

* * *

It was the early hours of Sunday morning when Sonny walked Ellie home after the dance. They planned to meet up and take a picnic to the woods, in a few hours after they'd slept.

'Can we meet outside the Officers' Mess about eleven?' Sonny said. 'Leave the picnic to me.'

He tilted her chin up with his finger and leaned towards her, touching her lips gently with his but before he could pull away, she'd put her arms around his neck, holding him tightly and in response, he'd kissed her hungrily. Waves of pleasure engulfed her as their bodies pressed against each other.

'Ellie!' he murmured.

She threw her head back, exulting in his butterfly kisses on her neck.

He'd found her mouth again and was kissing her when they were disturbed by the sound of someone inside the kitchen scraping a chair on the flagstones. They jumped apart guiltily. Ellie did up her collar, smartened her tie, then reluctantly said goodbye, watching him as he walked along the path, savouring the taste of him on her lips.

She didn't hear Kitty come home, although she knew it'd been much later because she'd lain awake for some time, reliving the feeling of holding Sonny close as they danced and of course, his kisses and caresses.

Everything seemed brighter, more colourful, more alive this morning and she couldn't wait until eleven o'clock came and she and Sonny would roam through the woods, spotting wildlife. He'd said he knew of a stream where they could eat their picnic and she tried to imagine them alone together.

She'd seen the desire in his eyes the previous evening and wondered how many girls he'd kissed. A man as handsome as Sonny would have had lots of girls. She remembered how she'd pulled him to her, kissing him urgently and passionately and wondered whether he'd been shocked.

He certainly hadn't seemed to mind,

responding with equal intensity. But so far, he'd behaved like a gentleman and there was no reason to suppose that later when they were alone, he'd treat her with anything other than respect. It was her own feelings she was afraid of.

She arrived at the station at ten-thirty but as soon as the guard waved her through, she could feel a change in atmosphere. Sonny saw her through the window and ran outside to her.

'Oh, Ellie, I'm so sorry, our picnic's off. All the pilots are confined to base. There's an op tonight and all leave's been cancelled. I don't know any more than that, but it's big, whatever it is. They wouldn't usually ask a pilot to fly on a mission that's so dangerous as the last op on his tour, but Squadron Leader's already talked to me and I've agreed to go. It's not fair on my crew if I don't. We're all used to each other and to spring a new pilot on them wouldn't be right.'

'I understand,' Ellie said, the colour and vibrancy of the day instantly draining away. 'Yes, of course. I expect I'll be called in too. You'll all need breakfast when you get home.'

She placed her hand on her chest, echoing his lucky ritual of touching the locket, and understanding her gesture, he took her hand and raised it briefly to his lips.

'As soon as I'm back we'll go on the picnic, I promise.' He turned and ran back into the mess.

Ellie started her shift early and the corporal was pleased to see her. The queues of people wanting meals seemed never-ending and Ellie wondered where everyone had suddenly come from. At least it took her mind off the important mission which would start at dusk.

One by one, the huge Wellingtons left the dispersal areas and lined up, their navigation lights winking red and green as they waited to lumber along the runway before sweeping up into the air and gradually disappearing into the gloom.

Ellie knew they'd be gone all night.

People were whispering that the bombers were headed on a hazardous mission over Berlin but no one except the senior officers knew for sure.

She wondered whether to go home and try to sleep but she was certain she wouldn't be able to relax until the planes — and specifically, P for Pip — had landed safely.

She spent most of the night in the Waafery, picking up magazines, flicking through them and then putting them down.

'Oh, there you are,' Kitty said brightly when she found Ellie. 'I've just got back from driving all sorts of top brass about. It's a big one tonight . . . Ellie, what's the matter? You look dreadful!'

'It's Sonny. It's the last op of his tour and . . . and I'm . . . '

'Oh, Ellie, I didn't realise you were so keen on him. Don't worry, darling, he'll be back. You'll see. Leo's gone as well. But you have to believe the best. Genevieve and Jess are on duty tonight.

We could go to the ops room and see if we can find out anything.'

'We're not allowed to bother them.'

'I know, but we might be able to get word to them to let us know when G for George and P for Pip are back.'

There was a small area next to the ops room where WAAFs could make a drink when there was a lull in the operation but on that night, everyone was too busy to make tea. Whenever the door opened, Ellie could see Genevieve and the other girls around the table, pushing wooden blocks over its surface with plotting rods to show the RAF men above them on a balcony, the number of aircraft, their position, height and bearings. Everyone was completely focused on their task and the strain was reflected in every face.

Kitty and Ellie made tea and silently delivered it to the workers who gulped quickly, not allowing it to take their minds off their work.

'K for King requesting permission to land,' one of the girls said.

'They're coming back,' Kitty said. 'They'll soon be home, you'll see.' She held Ellie's arm tightly and for the first time, Ellie realised that Kitty felt more for Leo than she'd admitted. She'd become so used to Kitty flirting with anyone — narrowly missing being placed on a charge for conduct unbecoming to a WAAF — that Ellie had assumed she wasn't very attached to Leo or anyone else. But the tension was evident in Kitty's eyes.

In the grey, dawn mist, Wellington after Wellington landed and taxied to the hangars. Weary men in flying suits, holding the emergency jackets they called Mae Wests, trudged towards their mess where they'd be questioned about their op, and then go for a huge breakfast before falling exhausted, into bed.

G for George had arrived and Ellie was glad to see the lines on Kitty's face soften as she smiled for the first time in hours. But still three aircraft hadn't returned.

L for London, Q for Queen and P for Pip. All still unaccounted for.

Then, L for London radioed in to say they'd been attacked over the Channel. Before the wireless operator could give exact coordinates, the signal failed.

Kitty held Ellie tightly and said nothing. They'd both known the crew members of L for London who now were either dead or fighting for their lives in the freezing waters of the Channel.

'Q for Queen's coming in,' one of the WAAF girls said. 'They're out of fuel. Stand by.'

Kitty and Ellie pulled their coats on as they ran outside into the early morning mist.

'There!' said Ellie, spotting the lights.

'It's coming in very steeply,' said Kitty, gripping Ellie and watching in horror. But at the last moment, the pilot pulled the nose up and the aircraft thudded on to the runway, chased by emergency vehicles. As it finally came to a standstill the girls could see the fuselage had been badly damaged by flak and the engine cowling had been torn away. But the crew emerged and were assisted down on to the ground. One of them was obviously wounded as the others gathered around him and helped him away.

'There's still hope, Ellie,' Kitty said.

'But if Q for Queen was out of fuel, P for Pip must be flying on fumes — if indeed it's still airborne,' Ellie wailed.

'Look!' said Kitty, 'Lights! Over there!'

From out of the mist, another Wellington appeared, ghostlike and silent.

'It's gliding!' Ellie said. 'It must be P for Pip.'

The markings on the fuselage weren't visible but it had to be Sonny and his crew. The crash tender, ambulance and fire tender were standing by, engines running, ready to assist if necessary.

As the plane veered around, following the runway, Ellie could see that indeed, it was P for Pip.

'Thank God. Now, please let him land safely.'

3

London

Kurt thought back to that night, so long ago, when he'd dreamed of flying out through Jack Rayment's attic window, up into the sky and back to Berlin to rescue his parents and sisters.

The dream had been particularly vivid and when he'd woken in the morning, his cheeks were wet with tears.

The lingering smell of vinegar and the chill on his scalp after having had his hair shaved off marked a turning point. Kurt decided he was not prepared to live like that for the rest of his life.

Jack had no choice; he had a family to keep. Without thinking about it, Kurt had looked to him as a role model, assuming he was tied by the same constraints. Despite Jack's unfailing optimism, it was unlikely he'd become the rich man he thought he ought to be.

But Kurt? He had no ties. And it was better if it remained like that. A single man could make his way — moving on if things didn't work out — but a husband and father had to stay and put up with whatever life threw at him.

Later that day, after doing his rounds of the second-hand clothes shops, he would go and see Mr Penhaligon in the bookshop next door and see if he could think of something Kurt could do with his life. After all, if he earned a better wage, he could help Jack and his family out as well.

Mr Penhaligon was poring over a newspaper when Kurt entered his shop and he slid his glasses on to the top of his head.

'Kurt, my boy! Finished your rounds already?'

Kurt nodded. 'There's more to do but I told Jack I'd come and see if you had any more deliveries to be made.'

'I've one book to go to Aldgate but I

was hoping you'd come in early so you could see it. Have you time to look now, and then wait while I wrap it?'

Kurt wasn't sure Jack would be happy if he delayed but Mr Penhaligon paid well and while they looked at the book, he could ask if he had any ideas. Perhaps he'd offer him a job. But that was doubtful. The book shop seemed to have lots of customers but not enough to be able to employ a full-time assistant.

Mr Penhaligon folded his newspaper and pushed it to one side, to make room for the book. It was *The Illustrated Guide To Modern Aircraft*.

'Look at those beauties,' Mr Penhaligon said, touching the illustrations of the planes which had flown during the Great War. 'The Sopwith F1 Camel,' he said shaking his head in wonder, 'arguably the RAF's most outstanding plane. But look at today's aircraft . . .' He turned to the end of the book. 'These are the RAF's finest now. From the news, it looks like Britain's going to need them all. And more besides. The RAF'll be important in the next war — you mark my words, Kurt, my boy.'

The next war. Kurt shuddered. The next war would see Germany, the land of his birth, pitted against Britain, the land which had offered him safety and which he'd now come to love — despite his hard life. The Nazis ruled in Germany, and had rejected him and his family. Britain had given him a home and a future and for that privilege, he would sacrifice his life.

He waited while Mr Penhaligon wrapped the book in brown paper. There was no need to ask the bookshop owner for his advice about Kurt's future. He'd already given it without knowing.

It could hardly be chance that the previous night he'd been dreaming about flying up into the night sky and that today, Mr Penhaligon had shown him a book of aircraft — indeed, a book of the future of warfare.

On Wednesday afternoon when Kurt

had time off, he knew exactly what he was going to do.

* * *

'You've done *what*?' Jack shouted when Kurt told him he'd signed up to join the RAF and was going to train to be a pilot.

Sylvia placed a hand on Jack's arm.

'It's for the best,' she said simply. 'And soon, our lives will be harder because there'll be a war on. They're already telling us what food'll be rationed.'

Jack nodded. 'Yes, I suppose you're right, my love. It's just that I felt that with Kurt's help, I was beginning to make headway. He's got such a good eye for cloth and the ladies love him. I know they keep back choice things for him. Now I'll be on my own again. And until the baby's born, you can't get out and do Kurt's job.'

'We'll manage — you'll see.'

Shortly before Kurt left for training

camp, a letter had arrived from Berlin. He hadn't recognised the handwriting on the envelope and he tore it open anxiously. This was the first letter he'd had from his home city for some time.

It was from a neighbour, Frau Pfister, whom Kurt remembered had often invited him into her apartment and served him large slices of delicious apple cake sprinkled with icing sugar. His mother had obviously given the neighbour Kurt's address in London and she'd written to tell him his mother and sisters had been taken away. She wasn't sure what had happened to them but she'd overheard one of the soldiers mention Ravensbrück, just north of Berlin, where there was a woman's concentration camp.

Kurt had wept after receiving that letter and vowed then that he would fight to free them.

His call-up papers had arrived shortly after.

He wasn't sure he'd be accepted as a pilot but so long as he was fighting against the Nazis, he'd do anything. Ground crew, air crew, he'd even sweep the floors so long as he felt he was fighting for Britain.

He worked hard during training, keeping focused on the thought that he'd be avenging his family. Finally he passed all his exams and received a commendation from his flying instructor.

'You're a first-class pilot, son. You've got nerves of steel and plenty of determination. Woe betide any Luftwaffe pilot who gets in your way.'

'Son' was how he was often referred to because when he'd joined up, he'd looked so young and skinny. His face had been pinched and his eyes had appeared too big for such a thin face. Eventually, he became known as Sonny. It was also a play on words as it sounded like Sunny, and that went well with his surname, Rayment.

Many pilots were given nicknames. Leo's real name was Daniel Vincent but someone had quipped that one young, naïve WAAF was 'about to wander into Daniel's lions' den' and after that, he'd been called Leo.

It pleased Kurt that he'd been given a nickname. It prevented anyone from remarking on his given name and wondering about its origin but more importantly, it showed he was one of the lads. He'd grown in stature, filling out as his muscles received the nourishment they'd lacked for so long and the exercise they needed, but he'd also grown in confidence. He was a man now, and it felt good to be able to send money to Jack and his family. He knew how much difference it made.

After a while, nothing about Kurt appeared to be German. No one would guess he wasn't British born and bred. Not that he'd lied to the authorities. They knew his paternal grandparents were German and he was born in Berlin. But it was the truth that his next of kin was Jack and his last address was Commercial Road, Whitechapel.

To his friends, he never spoke of

anything further back than that. If pressed, he spoke vaguely about Devon, implying his family came from the south-west. But it simply wasn't relevant. No one could have doubted his loyalties. He had a single-mindedness which was obvious to all.

Kurt hadn't told anyone why he was so driven. It was no one's business except his own that all the members of his family — if they were still alive — were in Nazi concentration camps. But everyone could see how determined he was and how skilled a pilot. His crew would do anything for him and they knew he felt the same about them. That was why, on this evening of the last operation of his first tour, he was flying P for Pip, rather than remaining at base, as many others would have done. After all, reaching twenty-nine successful operations was a great achievement and the thirtieth op could have been a routine flight, not this major offensive on Berlin. And then, he would have three months ground duty — unless he volunteered to get back into his Wellington.

He wouldn't have missed tonight's op for anything, although he wondered how he would feel when he was actually flying over the place of his birth, dropping bombs. He'd often imagined what it would be like — but now, to his surprise and dismay, he found his thoughts wandering. Not to Berlin, but to Ellie.

Her soft, blonde hair and the way she tilted her head when she looked up at him . . . It was disconcerting. He'd always maintained the utmost focus, but now . . .

Over the intercom, Tony Williams, the new rear gunner, spoke rapidly. 'Captain, there's an aircraft above us. I think it's a Messerschmitt. Turn starboard! He's right on top of us!'

As Kurt pulled the Wellington sharply to the right, he felt the stammer of Williams' guns from the rear gun turret and saw the Messerschmitt's bright tracer bullets stream past him.

'He's gone, Captain,' Tony reported.

Beads of sweat stood out on Kurt's forehead. That wasn't the closest shave he'd had by a large margin. He and his crew had faced worse. But he was appalled at how his mind had been drifting, not thinking about the mission but remembering how delicious it had been to kiss Ellie.

Concentrate! he told himself furiously. His men depended on him. That must not happen again!

If he couldn't keep his mind on the mission because of a girl, he needed to take advantage of the opportunity for ground duty and not risk his own life and those of his men. But he'd joined the RAF to fight — not to train others to do it for him.

Berlin was now below and he knew what he had to do. Pushing all thoughts of Ellie from his mind, he carried on with the mission. Kurt could see blazing factories and dropped his bombs over the fires, adding to the inferno and devastation. Searchlights criss-crossed the night sky, pinning planes in their beams for the anti-aircraft weapons which rattled away below them.

'Captain to crew: Mission completed. Returning to base,' Kurt said when his payload of bombs had been dropped.

He felt drained but there were still hours of flying before they got back to Holsmere.

Most of the journey was uneventful, although they had to avoid flak as they reached the coast, but at last they were over the Channel.

Nearly home, he thought. Any time now the cliffs of Dover would be in sight. He was exhausted.

Something caught his attention and with a shock, he saw three fighter planes above him, diving out of the clouds, spitting tracer bullets. Kurt swung the aircraft around, taking evasive action but sharp cracks rang out and the starboard engine began to shake and vibrate.

'Captain, there's petrol coming out of

tanks on the starboard wing.' It was Pat Harkness, the flight engineer.

From below, two Hurricanes swooped up towards the German planes firing at them as they turned and headed back across the Channel.

Thanks to the Hurricanes, the Germans had gone — but Kurt wasn't sure they'd have enough fuel to make it back to Holsmere.

'Captain to crew: The fuel indicator isn't working and I believe we may not have enough fuel to get us back to Holsmere, so I'm going to try to make it to RAF Hornchurch or Debden,' Kurt said into the intercom.

The Essex countryside, misty and grey in the dawn light, stretched out and a stiff breeze seemed to be carrying them along.

'Captain to crew: Holsmere's ahead, the fuel's pretty much gone but we can glide in. Hold tight.'

The fuselage had sustained more damage than Kurt had realised and he found that the starboard wheel would lower but not lock. He tried to raise the wheel so he could land on the belly of the plane but the wheel was stuck.

'Brace yourselves, it's going to be a rough landing,' he told the crew, anticipating a terrific impact as it hit the ground. After that, it was likely the plane would spin and possibly flip over.

However, Kurt managed to keep control of the aircraft as it landed, bounced up, sank down and bounced again. It veered sharply, leaving the runway and bumping over the grass. As he pressed the brakes as hard as he could, it came to a juddering halt.

It wasn't until Kurt tried to get out of the fuselage hatch he realised that when he'd been thrown sideways, he'd broken his arm. But mercifully, everyone else was unscathed.

* * *

'Ellie!' Genevieve called up the stairs to her bedroom. 'Sonny's here to see you!'

Ellie ran downstairs, expecting to

find him in the kitchen. She hadn't seen him since the ambulance had taken him away the morning he'd brought his Wellington in after the Berlin raid.

'He hasn't got time to come in,' Genevieve said when Ellie looked at her quizzically.

Sonny was standing a few feet from the door. He smiled at her but it wasn't the sort of smile he'd given her the last time he'd seen her. It was a sad, resigned smile and she felt something grip her heart and squeeze tightly.

She wanted to throw her arms around his neck to welcome him back, but with his arm in a sling, she dared not. And she could tell from his expression he wouldn't welcome such a gesture. Perhaps he was afraid she'd hurt his arm.

The look of relief on his face when she didn't throw herself at him, told her she'd been wise not to make a show of her affection.

She decided to keep things light. 'Well, Flight Lieutenant, you certainly gave us all a scare.'

He, too, adopted her playful tones, speaking in the renowned, understated way of a pilot.

'We had a spot of bother on the way back. Nothing too drastic. But we made it eventually.'

'Well, it's good to see you . . . '

He hesitated. 'It's good to be back . . . I came to tell you my leave's been put forward and I'm off to London in an hour.'

There would be no picnic as he'd promised once he'd got back. Not even a walk in the woods.

'I see,' she said. 'So, when will you be back?'

'I'm not sure. I'm thinking of going to a training camp as an instructor. While things are looking so bad for our men in France, we need to train fighter pilots to protect them.'

'Yes, of course.' She knew the Germans were pushing the Allies back towards the Channel and she also knew that Sonny hadn't wanted to train pilots before, he'd wanted to take part in flying operations. Something had changed his mind.

'I'll be on leave in London from tomorrow, too,' she said, hoping she was misreading the situation and that he'd jump at the chance to meet.

He remained silent.

'Where will you be?' she asked, trying to think of something to say which would engage him, something to keep him there, something to break down the seemingly insurmountable barrier which she could neither see, nor understand. 'Are you likely to be anywhere near St James's Square?'

He seemed to consider her question and there was a flicker — of what, she wasn't sure but it was as if he'd suddenly realised something. And then, just as rapidly, it was as if the light went out in his eyes and the remaining vestiges of affection he'd had for her had been snuffed out.

'No, sorry. I don't believe I will . . . Well, if you'll excuse me, I need to say goodbye to my men.' He was talking now as if they'd only just met.

He turned, paused and looked back.

'I'm sorry, Ellie . . . '

His tone was almost normal. Almost. Then he carried on down the path without looking back.

Ellie ran upstairs to her bedroom and looked out of the window towards the gap in the tall hedge through which she knew he would shortly come into view.

He walked quickly, his shoulders hunched and his head down. It was so unlike the Sonny she'd known a few days ago who stood proudly, his shoulders back and head held high.

Perhaps his arm was very painful. But she had a feeling it was more than physical pain. He'd come home from the Berlin raid a different man.

She stifled a sob.

'What is it, darling?' Kitty was in the doorway. 'I thought Sonny was taking you for a walk.'

'No, Kitty, he came to say goodbye.'

'You'll see him when he gets back.'

'No, I don't think he'll be coming back.'

'Surely not!'

'Something's changed, Kitty. I don't know what but whatever we had between us is over.'

Kitty held her tightly as the tears fell.

* * *

Saying goodbye to Ellie had been the hardest thing Kurt had ever done.

She'd smiled but he could tell his remoteness had hurt her and of course, the goodbye. How he'd longed to take her in his arms — well, his one good arm — and hold her close. But he couldn't. He mustn't. He owed it to his family to give every part of himself to fight the war and he couldn't do that while his mind was filled with images of Ellie.

During the last op his concentration hadn't been one hundred percent and if he couldn't give his all, then his men deserved a better captain — someone more reliable.

He'd seen her bottom lip tremble slightly and he'd almost changed his mind, recognising how unkind he was being. And then, she'd suggested they meet in London — in St James's Square — and his mind had flashed back to that day when he'd taken Karl Rosenberg's suitcase to that grand house and met the girl with the golden plaits.

When he first met Ellie at Holsmere, he'd thought she seemed familiar but assumed she'd been at one of the other bases where he'd been stationed. It hadn't occurred to him he'd met her as a schoolgirl in a wealthy part of London. He would never have guessed that the pretty, plump girl with blonde plaits and a fringe would turn into a shapely, beautiful woman with a heart-shaped face. Although the schoolgirl was called Eleanor, he was sure she had a double-barrelled surname — Eleanor Scott-Something? So the name Ellie Taylor, hadn't jogged his memory.

He couldn't imagine now, how he

because GC' — as she called Group Captain Hollingsworth, 'is very particular. He's kind, but, well . . . *particular*.'

Ellie noticed that Socrates, the cat, was looking rather fat and that GC seemed much thinner, but he greeted her cheerily and congratulated her on the marks she'd achieved.

One evening, there was a knock at the door at Larkrise Farm. Mrs Ringwood found a small, plump woman in a fur coat on the doorstep.

'I'd like to speak to Aircraftwoman Taylor, please,' she said.

'Who shall I say is asking for her?' Mrs Ringwood said.

'Mrs Hollingsworth. Group Captain Hollingsworth's wife.'

Mrs Ringwood shouted for Ellie and invited Mrs Hollingsworth in. When Ellie appeared, Mrs Hollingsworth asked for a word in private.

'Shall we go into the garden?' Ellie suggested, knowing Mrs Ringwood would not appreciate having to vacate her own kitchen.

'I shall be brief, Miss Taylor. I understand you are to be my husband's new secretary.'

'Yes.'

'Are you trustworthy, Miss Taylor?'

'Yes, Mrs Hollingsworth, I am.'

'I am going to have to trust you with certain information. But if I do so, you cannot divulge it.'

Ellie looked at the woman anxiously. This all sounded highly irregular.

'Well, I . . . '

Mrs Hollingsworth pressed on, 'My husband is not well. But he's as stubborn as a mule and while things are going so badly in this dreadful war, he won't take sick leave. He hides his illness and will continue to do so, for as long as he can — so long as he is of use to the RAF. That means from time to time, you may have to cover for him and you may have to administer his tablets. Occasionally, he's in so much pain, he can't open the bottle. Are you willing to take on this role? Cecily has done a wonderful job. Will you?'

'I . . . I'll do my best.'

'We're all doing our bit for this terrible war. But some of us are doing things which are not recognised jobs. My husband is doing what he's best at, and I am assisting him. Will you help me help him?'

'Yes, yes, of course.'

'And can my husband and I rely on your complete discretion in this delicate matter?'

'Yes. Definitely.'

'Thank you, Miss Taylor,' Mrs Hollingsworth said. 'Well, I'll leave you to enjoy your free time.'

As Ellie watched her walk away down the path, she wondered what could be wrong with GC. It must be something serious for him not to simply get treatment. Perhaps there was no treatment.

It certainly made sense of why GC couldn't eat large meals and why he'd lost weight. On one occasion, she'd seen him grimace with pain and clutch his stomach. Despite Mrs Hollingsworth's stony expression and cool tone, Ellie had seen her eyes fill with tears and the nervous swallow as she'd said her husband wasn't well.

As soon as Cecily left, in a week and a half, Ellie would do her best to support GC and to assist him in his work.

The following morning, however, when Ellie arrived at the office, the telephone was ringing. It was Cecily's husband. She'd fallen and had been taken into hospital where she'd stay until the doctors were sure the pregnancy was safe.

Ellie was now in charge of Group Captain Hollingsworth's office.

* * *

'Come on, Ellie, it'll do you good!' Kitty said. 'A dance is just what you need.'

But Ellie was exhausted. It wasn't that GC worked her very hard — she could handle all the office work easily.

But the emotional burden placed on her by GC's illness was draining her.

Kitty wasn't helping. Not that it was her fault but the first time she and Leo broke up, the sleepwalking had started. And the night terrors, when Kitty woke, drenched in sweat and incoherent with fear, until Ellie held her gently and brought her back to reality.

Kitty had been mortified when she'd woken in the kitchen with no memory of having got out of bed or of Ellie trying to coax her back.

She'd begged Ellie not to tell anyone.

'They'll think I'm mad. I couldn't bear it if I was discharged.'

Another secret for Ellie to keep. And even worse, it was affecting her sleep. Often, during the day, she felt desperately tired.

She hoped that when Kitty and Leo got back together, the sleepwalking and disturbance would stop, and it did. But it wasn't long before Kitty was furious with Leo for flirting with a very pretty WAAF who worked in the op room with Genevieve. Kitty then took her revenge with one of the pilots. So the last thing Ellie wanted was to go dancing. She longed to forget the war, the missing pilots, GC's illness and Kitty and Leo's bad behaviour. And she wanted to sleep.

Kitty persuaded Genevieve and Jess to go with her to the dance but Ellie was adamant.

* * *

The following morning there was a strained atmosphere at breakfast.

'What happened last night?' Ellie asked.

'Well,' said Genevieve nervously, 'Kitty and Leo are back together and . . . Sonny's back.'

'Oh!' Ellie's heart jumped.

'I know you and he . . . well, it's just that Kitty and Leo are going to the ENSA performance on Friday and . . . well, Sonny asked me to go. Would you mind?'

'Mind?' Ellie said, trying to keep her voice normal. 'Of course not. He's nothing to me now. I hope you have a lovely time.'

It wasn't the truth, but she would do her best to make it true. It was simply a question of hardening her heart. After all, how much pain could a heart take before it simply stopped feeling anything at all? Like a puddle slowly freezing from the outside inwards, her heart was turning to ice.

Love was overrated. Look at her parents. She'd thought they were happy but they were living separate lives. Kitty and Leo were made for each other but for some reason, as soon as they got together, one of them couldn't help looking elsewhere and hurting the other. And Sonny . . . She'd thought they had something special but it turned out to be nothing at all.

And even when love worked out, like GC and his wife, who were obviously deeply committed to each other, slowly they were being prised apart because although neither of them had told Ellie, she knew that GC was dying. He was fighting for his country and paying with his life.

So, why on earth would anyone make any effort at all to fall in love?

Yes, she wished Genevieve and Sonny well, if that was what they wanted.

* * *

The performance by the Entertainments National Service Association, more popularly known as ENSA, was just what everyone at RAF Holsmere needed.

Operation Dynamo, the evacuation of Allied troops from Dunkirk had taken place a few weeks before at the end of May and the beginning of June. The nation rejoiced at the safe return of the troops whose situation had looked desperate indeed, being trapped on the beaches in northern France by the advancing German army.

The new Prime Minister, Winston

Churchill, had praised the courage and tenacity of those in their Little Ships — as the private vessels of all kinds had been dubbed — who'd assisted the Royal Navy. But he'd been careful to point out that wars were not won by evacuations.

Britain still had a long way to go if it was to make headway against Hitler's troops who'd marched right through Holland, Belgium and France.

'The Battle of France is over,' Churchill declared. 'The Battle of Britain is about to begin.'

The Führer's next step would surely be to take Britain and it seemed he planned to do that with his mighty Luftwaffe. By July, German aircraft had started bombing British ports and RAF airfields, trying to destroy Britain's air force. He was convinced the German pilots and their planes were superior to anything Churchill had to offer. In his opinion, it was only a matter of time until the Battle of Britain would be won — by the Germans.

During Kurt's leave, he'd spent some time in Whitechapel with Jack. Kurt smiled when he heard that Sylvia, the new baby girl and two youngest boys had been evacuated to the south-west. At last, he really had family living in Devon!

It was also good to know they were in the relative safety of the countryside. Benjamin had left school and was working with Jack. The money Kurt sent each week had made a big difference, and the basement workshop now boasted three machines and a part-time worker. But of course, the war made things difficult for everyone.

Kurt then spent a few weeks training new recruits but after the Dunkirk evacuation and the beginning of the attacks on RAF bases, it became clear to him that his time would be better spent using his flying experience taking part in bombing missions over Germany and destroying ammunitions and aircraft factories, rather than training men and sending them out after a short course in flying to take part in dogfights with the Luftwaffe. He knew that many of those he'd taught to fly had already lost their lives.

Leo had been delighted to see Kurt back at Holsmere, as had his crew. It was obvious, however, that things had changed since that day he'd said goodbye to Ellie and gone on leave.

RAF Holsmere had been attacked several times. One raid had severely damaged the Officers' Mess and destroyed several Wellingtons. Personnel had died too — one navigator, six ground crew and three WAAF aircraftwomen. Many others had been badly wounded.

'Is Kitty all right?' he'd asked Leo.

'Yes, and just in case you're wondering, old chap, so are Ellie, Genevieve and Jess.'

Kurt was pleased Leo had offered the information because he'd wanted to know about Ellie but wouldn't have asked. Leo had already quizzed him about finishing with Ellie.

'You two are made for each other,

Sonny. What's wrong with you?'

But there was no going back. He owed his crew his full concentration. If he was with Ellie, he couldn't guarantee that. And there was the chance Ellie would remember they'd already met. She'd surely be disgusted at the memory and the fact that he'd deceived her about his past.

Leo had kept on at him. 'Come to the dance on Saturday. Ellie might be there, you could just have a few dances . . . you never know where that'll lead.'

He'd repeatedly refused but Leo kept on and reluctantly, he'd finally agreed to go.

Ellie, however, wasn't at the dance.

His head told him it was a good thing she wasn't there although his heart felt heavy.

Kitty and Leo had gone to the dance together and for a change, it looked as though they might actually be leaving together. Genevieve and Jess had gone to the dance too and out of politeness, Kurt danced with both of them.

No, not out of politeness; he knew they would probably both mention Ellie, and he would hear about her even if she wasn't there. It was like twisting a knife in a wound but he couldn't stop.

Jess had an early shift the following day so she'd excused herself early, leaving Genevieve, who, Kurt discovered was a very pleasant, bubbly girl. He wondered why he'd never noticed her before, but then, he'd had eyes for no one other than Ellie. Genevieve couldn't have been more different from Ellie, with her smooth, dark bob and her smouldering eyes. She was bright, too, and had a keen sense of humour.

She told him about living with the irrepressible Kitty and how she annoyed quiet Jess with her noise and her exuberance.

'It's hard to understand how Ellie gets on so well with Kitty,' Genevieve said. 'They're almost complete opposites. Kitty's getting worse — she's narrowly missed being on a charge several times but she always seems to talk her way out of it. And Ellie . . . '

He hadn't liked to say 'Yes, what about Ellie?' He knew his voice would be too eager. Instead, he'd waited to see if Genevieve would continue.

'Well, Ellie has become very serious since she's come back from training. She seems to love her job and she's fiercely protective of Group Captain Hollingsworth. She won't hear anything said against him. It's strange, really. Kitty started teasing her, saying she was falling in love with a man who was old enough to be her father and Ellie shouted at her. I've never seen Ellie so angry. But at least it stopped Kitty! She hasn't mentioned the group captain since.'

Genevieve sighed. 'But Ellie is spending too much time at work. She often works well past the end of her shift. I go by the office when I've finished and she usually tells me she's too busy to leave. It's a shame she didn't come tonight. She needs to relax a bit. Perhaps she'll come to the ENSA concert on Friday.'

Leo gave him the thumbs-up several times when he saw Kurt dancing with Genevieve and at the end of the evening, he'd walked her home and suggested he take her to the ENSA performance the following Friday. His first op was scheduled for Monday.

It hadn't been necessary for either of them to mention there was a good chance he might not make the date because he'd be killed before Friday — it was understood by both of them. The Battle of Britain was raging; no one knew if they'd be alive next day, let alone in five days' time.

There had been a raid on the base on Wednesday but it seemed it was a lone German Junkers Ju 88 which had dived on the airfield, strafing the Wellingtons and any staff unlucky enough to be outside. Anti-aircraft fire had soon seen him off and there was a cheer when the flak hit him and the pilot could be seen parachuting down, to land somewhere in the Essex countryside. The aircraft tumbled out of the sky and an explosion could be heard from a few miles away.

'They'll soon round him up,' Leo said. 'His war is over.'

Privately, Kurt was glad the pilot had escaped. He might send bombs raining down on Germany but he had no wish to kill. Simply to stop the killing — and that wouldn't happen until Hitler and his generals were stopped.

Two Wellingtons were lost during bombing missions that week but Leo and Kurt returned unscathed. As usual when they lost fellow pilots, they met at the Wild Boar and toasted the men who would never return.

When Kurt had first seen how aircrew reacted when comrades were lost, he thought it heartless. It was as if no one cared. Everyone was intent on pretending that all was fine — they went to the pub, they laughed and joked. It seemed inhuman.

Then he'd realised how important it was that they each maintained a veneer of nonchalance and encouraged the view they were indifferent to the dangers they faced each time their aircraft lifted off the runway. It was an act. But it had to be kept up and Kurt joined in, knowing he couldn't afford to show the slightest emotion because once he started, it would be impossible to stop.

* * *

Kitty, Genevieve and Jess tried to persuade Ellie to go to the ENSA concert but she refused, until she discovered GC would be there. At least she could keep an eye on him. He'd grown even thinner and his eyes were now sunken but he kept on working. His wife had arranged to have an armchair delivered to his office so he could nap when he was tired, and Ellie stopped anyone going in if she thought he was asleep, telling them GC was in the middle of an important telephone call and they should come back in half an hour.

When GC wasn't napping, Socrates the cat slept on the chair and it became a joke which Ellie encouraged that the group captain was so fond of his cat, he had a special chair for him. Better they thought GC too soft on his cat than that anyone guessed how ill he was.

Still, Ellie couldn't believe that none of the top brass knew. If they did, they seemed happy to go along with the subterfuge. The terrible attacks on Britain by the Luftwaffe, who were intent on destroying the RAF, needed every experienced man it could muster. And Group Captain Hollingsworth was one of the very best.

The concert was a great success, raising morale which had been slipping since the Battle of Britain had begun. Comedians parodied Hitler and the Nazi officials, making everyone laugh. Sophia Vanelli, the rising young pianist, played and then accompanied a choir who sang poignant songs which caused the audience to fall silent, followed by upbeat songs of defiance and patriotism. During the finale of *We're Going to Hang Out the Washing on the Siegfried Line*, everyone joined in, swaying from side to side.

Kurt walked Genevieve home and at the door, he kissed her cheek. She was a lovely girl, but . . .

But what? he wondered as he walked back to the base. *But I've switched off my emotions so effectively, I now can't feel anything.*

Was that true?

He'd decided some time ago, the best thing to do was not think of Ellie at all.

But now he thought he'd test his emotions by bringing her to mind and yes, it still seemed to slice into him like a knife. He hadn't managed to switch off his emotions at all. He knew that for him, it was either Ellie, or no one.

So it must be no one.

However, it seemed Ellie had moved on. Every so often, he'd glanced at her during the performance and seen that mostly, she wasn't watching the show, she was looking at Group Captain Hollingsworth. Not that he'd returned her attention. He'd thoroughly enjoyed the concert.

Kurt could see warmth and softness in Ellie's eyes. Something he couldn't describe. And if Genevieve's words were anything to go by, it seemed that as unlikely as it appeared, Ellie had found a new object for her affections, even if her feelings weren't reciprocated. Why should they be? Group Captain Hollingsworth was married. But this was wartime and people did rash things.

Genevieve had invited Kurt to her birthday celebration at the Wild Boar the following Wednesday. He'd hesitated, knowing it likely that Ellie would be there but, in the end, he decided he had to move on, just as Ellie had. And Genevieve seemed so keen that he be there.

On Monday, he went into Chelmsford to buy Genevieve a present. He had no idea what she liked because he didn't know her well but there wasn't a great choice in the shops anyway.

As he passed a jeweller's window, he

saw a delicate silver heart-shaped charm. He hadn't intended to buy anything so personal but if he didn't hurry, he'd miss the last bus.

On the way home, he touched his chest, pressing the heart-shaped locket his mother had given him, against his skin. His good luck charm. It had obviously been in his mind when he'd spotted the silver heart.

However, he began to wonder if he hadn't made a great mistake. To him, hearts meant luck. But to others, they represented love. Genevieve would understand that, wouldn't she? Of course, love hadn't been on his mind. After all, they'd only been out together once.

Best to make sure, he thought and decided that before she opened it, he'd tell her about his lucky charm, so she understood.

* * *

On Monday, while Kurt was strolling around Chelmsford looking for a birthday gift, Group Captain Hollingsworth collapsed at work.

Ellie heard a crash and rushed into his office to find him sprawled on the floor, unconscious. She called an ambulance and telephoned Mrs Hollingsworth, suggesting she go straight to the hospital. Ellie accompanied him, holding his hand and willing him to open his eyes.

He'd become like a father to her, she realised. Someone to look up to and to care for. When she'd first become his secretary, he'd been patient with the few mistakes she'd made and had shown compassion when he'd found her in floods of tears after dealing with so many records of fine young men who'd arrived at the station, fresh-faced and eager to show the Luftwaffe their newly-acquired skills, only to fail to return from their first op.

GC had told her that when he was alone, he too, shed tears at the wanton and cruel waste of life. But while they were at work, they had to be calm and efficient — for everyone's sake.

At the hospital, Group Captain Hollingsworth was pronounced dead and Mrs Hollingsworth clung to Ellie. The two women sobbed.

If GC had thawed Ellie's heart slightly, the pain of losing such a lovely man had now frozen it solid.

* * *

The funeral was a sombre affair, well attended by those at Holsmere as well as many of the senior officers in the RAF.

Ellie was distraught. It was so unfair. He'd been a fine man, trying to look after a station of good men and women, many of whom had gone to their deaths under his command. At the end of the burial, she realised she had no more tears to shed. She was empty. She was beyond pain.

Ellie watched the mourners leave the graveside with a feeling of unreality, as if she was completely detached — as if she didn't belong. It was similar to the sensation she'd had at the ENSA concert a few days before when three of the actors had performed a sketch while wearing masks. It had remained in her mind because during the last few months, she'd felt that GC and his wife had been wearing masks that hid their sadness while they pretended to the world that all was normal.

Life, Ellie decided, is a place where everyone is acting, simply going through the motions of living.

Everything seemed utterly pointless.

Looking around the mourners, she wondered what other troubles were hidden behind masks.

She watched as one of the most senior officers present at the funeral made his way towards Kitty. Ellie wondered if Kitty was about to be reprimanded as the man looked very stern. Indeed, her friend appeared very uncomfortable but to her surprise, the man smiled, patted Kitty's shoulder and walked away.

'My father — Air Marshal Spencer,' Kitty said when she saw Ellie's puzzled expression. 'I'm amazed he recognised me,' she added bitterly.

Ellie noticed Sonny still at the graveside, head bowed. He looked up and their eyes met, then giving a slight nod, he turned and walked away.

* * *

'Well, go on, Sonny!' Leo said, shoving Kurt forward. 'Give the birthday girl her present!'

'I . . . ' Kurt said, not wanting to hand the gift-wrapped box over without explaining that it was a lucky heart charm and not a romantic declaration. But Leo had whipped it out of his hand and given it to Genevieve.

She opened it excitedly but her brows drew together, when she saw the silver heart charm. 'It's beautiful, Sonny. Really beautiful,' she said.

Putting the lid back on the box, she slipped it into her pocket, then took the gift that Kitty gave her and opened it.

Genevieve drew Kurt to one side and asked if she could talk to him outside the pub, out of earshot of the others.

'The charm, it's not — ' Kurt began, but Genevieve placed her finger on his lips.

'Thank you, but I know what it doesn't mean, Sonny, and I think it best I don't accept it.'

'Why?'

'Because I don't think I know you well enough for you to give me a heart. And we'll never know each other well enough because I'm leaving. The others don't know yet because I didn't want to spoil my celebration, but I'll be going soon.'

'Where are you going?'

'I can't say. And I'd be grateful if you can keep this to yourself until I announce it. But I've thought for some time I could do more. I'm fluent in French and I can be of use . . . elsewhere.'

'Elsewhere? You don't mean France?'

'Shh! It means I'll go wherever I'm sent. And do whatever's necessary.'

'Genevieve!' He'd known she was a bright, active girl but if his guess was right, she was telling him she was about to become an agent working for Britain behind enemy lines in France, Holland, Belgium or wherever she was sent.

'So, you see, I can't take your heart,' she said. 'I never had it and I never will.'

'Please, Genevieve, it was meant more as a good luck charm. I'd have explained that if Leo had given me the chance. But now, more than ever, I do sincerely wish you luck. Please keep it.'

She raised the lid to look at the tiny silver heart.

'Thank you, Sonny. You're a good, kind man.' She thought for a moment. Replacing the lid, she said, 'Yes, thank you — I will accept it as a good luck charm. And when I look at it, I'll think of you.'

* * *

Group Captain Jennings took over Ellie's office and she found him dedicated, fair and appreciative of all her hard work and determination. She missed Group Captain Hollingsworth but there was plenty to keep her occupied and at least now, she could do her job without having the added worry of looking out for her senior officer's health.

The Luftwaffe had stepped up their attacks on airfields, still believing they could crush the RAF. For the personnel at Holsmere it was a harrowing time with frequent aerial bombardment causing destruction and death. And of course, there were many losses among the air crew, as the Wellington bombers continued to fly missions over Germany.

One evening as Ellie was drifting off to sleep, Kitty ran in and sat on the end of her bed.

'Ellie, darling, wake up, you'll never guess what! Genevieve and Jess are both leaving.'

'Leaving? What? Where are they going?'

'Well, Genevieve's going to London to do some special clerical work.'

'Genevieve doing clerical work? She's such an active person. She can't sit still for a minute. And she hates being indoors.'

'I know. It all sounds improbable although she did say something about using her language skills. She's fluent in French and I think she speaks some German too. I was wondering if she's going off to do something active . . . and dangerous.'

'Well, that sounds more like Genevieve. Is Jess going with her?'

'No, she's going to some place called Bletchley Park. I think it's in Buckinghamshire or Berkshire. She's also going to do some sort of clerical work. It all sounds very odd to me.'

Ellie sat up, wide awake now. 'Are you sure?'

'Of course I'm sure, they just told me they'll be leaving at the end of the week. Poor Sonny.'

'Why 'poor Sonny'?' Ellie asked.

'He was obviously rather taken with Genevieve.'

'Was he? I didn't know. What makes you say that? I thought he'd only taken her out once.'

'He bought her a beautiful silver charm in the shape of a heart for her birthday.'

'Oh! She didn't show me.'

Kitty thought for a moment. 'Well, perhaps she thought you might still have feelings for him. You know how thoughtful she is.'

'Oh, well, I don't still have feelings for him,' Ellie said firmly.

Kitty patted her hand.

'No,' she said. 'You don't seem to have feelings about anything any more.'

'What on earth do you mean?'

'You're much tougher than you used to be.'

'I've just grown up,' Ellie said, throwing the covers back and reaching for her dressing gown. 'Well, I'd better go and congratulate Jess and Genevieve on their new posts.'

Shaking her head, Kitty followed her downstairs.

* * *

Ellie lay awake for a long time, Kitty's words, wistful and regretful, whirling in her brain.

You're much tougher than you used to be.

Tougher.

Well, it was true. Ellie was tougher and harder. But she found it easier to cope if she kept herself remote from everything. She was efficient and reliable in her work, and she knew that Group Captain Jennings had come to rely on her.

It wouldn't help anyone if she became emotional about her job or her private life. And if a conversation Ellie had accidentally overheard was anything to go by, Sonny was discovering the same thing regarding his attachment to Genevieve.

She'd been returning from Chelmsford on the bus and had heard two

RAF men sitting at the back mention Sonny. Ralph Baker, the navigator, and Tony Williams, the rear-gunner, were returning from a trip to the cinema and were discussing their last op.

' . . . he seems to be taking more risks. I don't like it,' said Ralph.

'I know,' replied Tony. 'I've only just got engaged and I'd really like to see my wedding day next month. I used to feel safe with the captain . . . well, as safe as you can be up in a Wimpy, being shot at by the Hun. Captain was always driven, but now . . . it's like he doesn't care about himself. And that means we're all in danger too.'

Everyone knew Sonny was an exceptional pilot. For his crew to be discussing him now, expressing their doubts, was quite unexpected and Ellie had been shocked. It was out of character — but perhaps he'd known about Genevieve going away and it had affected him deeply.

It confirmed her belief that the best course of action was to remain completely detached. And the only way Ellie knew how to do that, was not to let anything close enough to risk melting her frozen heart.

* * *

The Germans continued their dreadful attacks on British airfields and radar stations. However, despite RAF aircraft often being outnumbered during aerial engagements and suffering heavy losses, the Luftwaffe couldn't gain the air superiority it needed before Hitler's planned invasion of Britain could take place.

By the middle of August, the Luftwaffe were carrying out attacks against the radar stations which were so effective in giving warnings of their impending attacks — but they'd suffered dreadful losses too. One day, during the heaviest fighting of the war, they lost seventy-five aircraft. In Germany, it became known as Black Thursday.

Nevertheless, their bombardment continued and Holsmere was targeted repeatedly. Damage to infrastructure was repaired as soon as possible and despite the Luftwaffe's best efforts, it remained operational, still sending out its Wellington bombers to Germany.

'Not again!' Ellie muttered as she entered the ops block with a file for Group Captain Jennings and the air raid warning came over the tannoy. As she went out towards the shelter, enemy planes could already be seen and bombs were dropping.

The first explosion was so close, it hurled Ellie backwards into the ops block, the smell of dust and fumes filling her nostrils. She got up and staggered to the ops room where amidst the dust and falling plaster, she could see the WAAFs on duty with their tin hats on. The plotters were listening attentively to the voices from their headphones, moving their pieces over the table. Everyone else was in position, working intently.

The voice coming over the tannoy was directing everyone to take shelter but still the staff in the ops room remained. There was an atmosphere of tension, yet everyone carried on — only the occasional glance up at the ceiling when yet another explosion was heard from outside betrayed their nervousness. Their voices were raised so they could make themselves heard over the din but Ellie didn't detect any panic, just calm efficiency and she suddenly realised why no one was running for shelter. Their squadron of Wellington bombers was returning from a raid — and their arrival was imminent. But how could they land if everyone left their posts and didn't guide them in?

Group Captain Jennings caught sight of her at the door and made gestures for her to take cover, although he remained on the balcony with his men, overlooking the table on which the plotters moved their pieces representing aircraft in their area. No doubt, they could see how close the Wellingtons were.

Ellie decided to take the GC's advice. After all, she couldn't help anyone in the ops room.

Outside, oily, black smoke billowed across the airfield and runway and Ellie could see that behind her, the sergeants' mess had been hit. There were glass shards and piles of bricks where a wall had been. She could see tables and chairs covered in debris inside the damaged building.

The bombs were still falling as a Junkers Ju 88 dived towards the hangars with its characteristic scream which made the hairs on the back of Ellie's neck stand on end. It strafed a Wellington which was grounded for repair as well as the group of flight mechanics who were running to find shelter. The bullets kicked up dust as they struck the ground, chasing the men as they ran.

Ellie held the tin hat on her head and pushed the heels of her hands to her ears. It was deafening. She hesitated, wondering whether to run, take her chance and hope the pilot of the Junkers, who'd strafed the mechanics, didn't notice her.

She looked up and saw that at long last, he'd gone — and the other enemy aircraft were following it.

At first, Ellie thought she could see two of the squadron's Wellingtons returning from their mission but as they carried on over the airfield in pursuit of the German aircraft, she realised they were RAF Hurricanes, probably scrambled from nearby North Weald aerodrome.

Her relief was short-lived when she looked at the destruction left behind by the Luftwaffe, especially to the runway.

The Wimpys! How would they land?

There were craters and unexploded bombs on the section of the runway closest to her, and there were bound to be more at the far end where the aircraft would begin to land. The advice was that such bombs should be avoided by a margin of about twenty-five yards. That was easy for a person on foot, but the pilots wouldn't see the unexploded bombs until they were on top of them.

Ellie ran to the closest hangar and inside, found a bundle of red flags which she grabbed. Holding her tin hat in place with one hand, she ran to the first unexploded bomb and carefully placed one of the marker flags next to it, then moved on to the next bomb, working her way across the runway.

She'd marked all the bombs when the all-clear sounded and she saw people running to the craters with spades, preparing to fill them in, ready for the return of the Wimpys.

The unmistakable sound of a Wellington arriving could be heard as she was joined by Group Captain Jennings, armed with a spade.

'Jolly good show, Ellie. Your quick thinking and bravery will have saved dozens of lives today.'

* * *

Many people received injuries during the attack on Holsmere but miraculously, there had been no fatalities. Unusually, although one of the aircraft had sustained flak damage, all the air crew had returned unscathed too.

There was a mood of optimism across the station. The RAF — which Hitler had assumed he would easily destroy — was inflicting significant damage on the Luftwaffe. In addition, the British were building and replacing aircraft at a faster rate than the Germans. Hitler certainly hadn't lost but he wasn't winning either. And the longer the Battle of Britain lasted, the more victory slipped from his grasp.

Whoever wasn't working a shift that evening was at the Wild Boar in the village. The pilots and their teams bought drinks and toasted the staff of the ops room, who'd courageously guided them home — and of course Ellie, who'd marked the areas of runway to avoid, ensuring they knew where it was safe to land.

Ellie was embarrassed at the fuss — it was something she thought anyone would do knowing the Wimpys were about to land. At the time, she hadn't thought about the danger she was in.

Leo had hugged her and was now chatting to one of the WAAF plotters who'd been in the ops room when it was being bombarded. Kitty, having seen Leo flirting outrageously with the petite blonde, had linked arms with one of the pilots and was listening intently to his every word. From time to time, she saw Kitty glance over her shoulder towards Leo and she was certain Leo was keeping an eye on Kitty.

Why don't they just stop playing with other people and stay together? Ellie wondered.

Intent on watching Kitty, she didn't see Sonny slide into the seat next to her.

'I just wanted to say thank you for your bravery on the runway,' he said. 'And I wanted to . . . ' He paused; there was so much noise. 'Could we go outside? Just for a few minutes.'

She got up to follow him. Two pilots, arms around each other, were singing *Doing The Lambeth Walk* at the tops of their voices and someone was picking out the notes on the piano.

They crossed the road to a bench on the village green, far away from the raucous noise of the bar. The moon was peeping over the horizon.

'That was very brave of you to mark all those unexploded bombs, Ellie,' he said.

'Not really. I don't remember feeling brave, or even scared. I don't think I was thinking about anything other than the fact that you were all coming back to a runway full of bombs.'

'Well, the lads and I are grateful anyway.' He paused. 'Too many good men and women have already died. By the way, I haven't yet offered my condolences for the loss of Group Captain Hollingsworth. I saw you at the funeral but I had to leave straight after the burial. I understand he was very special to you.'

Ellie sighed. 'He was a lovely man — just like a father to me. I suppose that's strange since I only worked for him for a short while, but he was so caring. I can't tell you how sad it was to find out he was terminally ill. He showed real bravery. He hid his condition so he could carry on working and I saw how much that cost him. Poor Mrs Hollingsworth. The two of them were so devoted. It was a tragedy.'

'Oh, Ellie, I'm so sorry . . . I'm afraid . . . well, I assumed you had a different relationship.'

Ellie stood up, her face showing her outrage.

'How dare you, that's monstrous!' She began to walk off and he rose quickly and followed her.

'Ellie, I'm sorry, I really am! Please forgive me. I'd seen you out and about with him and it was obvious you cared deeply. I mistook that for something else. Please, Ellie, there's so much sadness and anger in the world. Can't we be friends? I've lost too many friends already.'

She stopped and turned slowly. 'Yes, I suppose you're right.' They sat down again on the bench.

'You must miss Genevieve a lot,' she said.

'Genevieve?' He sounded surprised.

'Well, I hear you were very close to her.'

'Not really. She was a nice girl but I wasn't close to her at all.'

'But Kitty said you gave her a charm for her birthday. A heart-shaped charm.'

'Ah, yes.' He looked at the ground. 'I think I may have made a bit of a mistake with that.'

'A mistake?'

'Well, d'you remember my good luck charm?'

'The heart-shaped locket of your mother's?'

'Well, for me, hearts have become inextricably linked with luck. I thought it would bring Genevieve good fortune.

I didn't really consider it a romantic present. Genevieve was very embarrassed and didn't want to take it but I explained to her and in the end, she accepted it in the spirit I'd intended. So, you see how very foolish I am with women. As Leo says, I'm completely useless and he's right. He's never let me forget how I treated you.'

'But . . . I assumed I'd upset you somehow.'

He sighed. 'No, you didn't do anything wrong. It was me. I was getting too fond of you. That was the trouble. I found I was thinking of you when I should've been concentrating on flying. It wasn't fair on the lads. And then, of course . . . '

'What?'

He stared at the ground, then sighed again.

'Well, I might as well make a proper job of humiliating myself . . . ' He swallowed. 'My name isn't Sonny Rayment or even Kurt Rayment — '

'It's Kurt Rosenberg,' she said.

'How d'you know?' His eyes opened wide.

'I have access to the files of all the personnel on Holsmere. I had to prepare something for GC once and I saw your records. I noticed your name and that you came from Berlin as a refugee.'

'You knew?' He looked at her in horror. 'Why didn't you say something?'

'What difference does it make? Sonny or Kurt. Rayment or Rosenberg. I like them all as names. And if you think I might doubt your loyalty to Britain because you were born in Germany, you've proved over and over which side you're on. There's just one thing I'd like to know . . . '

'Yes?'

'That day we met in London, when you came to St James's Square to return that suitcase to its rightful owner, you said you'd try to come back on Sunday to see me. Did you ever intend to?'

Kurt groaned. 'Oh, you remember

our meeting too?' He put his head in his hands.

'Of course! Although I must admit, I didn't put two and two together until I saw your name in your records. There was something familiar about your eyes, but you were a boy when I first met you and then when I met you the second time, you were a man. When did you first recognise me?'

'Not until the day you mentioned St James's Square. I didn't think you knew we'd met before and I was keen to get away from you before you remembered. I'm sure you'll know why.'

'No. Actually, I have no idea,' Ellie said.

'But you must do! Don't you remember how disgusted you were?'

'Disgusted? What on earth d'you mean?' Ellie drew her brows together, trying to picture their first meeting in her mind's eye. 'I remember we were talking outside my house and then I saw my mother at the window. I knew she'd be furious if she saw me talking to a boy in the street, so I ran up the steps and let myself in the front door . . . but disgusted? All I remember is being shocked at seeing my mother.'

'I didn't realise. I thought you'd seen something quite different.'

He told her about arriving home and finding the house reeking of vinegar because all the boys had head lice and how he'd been so ashamed, assuming she'd seen them in his hair.

'Oh, Sonny! I'm so sorry. How awful for you.'

'Well, as it happens, that day was pivotal in my life. It spurred me on to join the RAF which turned out to be the best thing for me. Every cloud . . . '

'Isn't it strange how things happen over which we've no control and yet they shape our lives? So much has gone on over the last few months, I feel like a different person.'

'You seem different from the girl I walked home that time.'

'Kitty says I'm tougher and harder now.'

'Perhaps we're all harder. How can you be otherwise during a war which has resulted in so much senseless loss of life?'

A cold breeze blew across the village green and Ellie shivered.

'Would you like to go back in the pub?' Kurt asked.

'No, I think I'll go home now.'

'Would you allow me to walk you home?'

'I'd like that very much indeed, thank you.'

They walked along the road and Ellie was reminded of the last time he'd accompanied her from the village to Larkrise Farm.

How long ago that seemed. How naïve she'd been, how unprepared for life. Hatred and love had always seemed so black and white and if the fairy tales of her childhood were to be believed, love always conquered all. Now, she knew that with each fresh atrocity that was committed during this terrible war, hatred thrived.

And love? Well, there were many types which all seemed to involve opening oneself up to heartache and pain.

She thought again of her parents, of GC and Mrs Hollingsworth. Kitty and Leo fell in and out of love — neither able to commit to the other.

And so many good people who'd been part of her world had been blown from the skies, crushed under fallen masonry or riddled with bullets.

No, it was too painful to consider getting close to anyone. And yet . . . Walking next to Sonny, sharing the calls of the nocturnal animals and the silvery moonlight with him, it seemed so right.

'Are you thinking about the last time we did this?' he asked.

'Yes.'

'Me too. I really enjoyed your company . . . perhaps . . . we could spend more time together?'

'Perhaps . . . ' It wasn't what she wanted to hear. And yet . . . This evening, in the moonlight, being with

Sonny was perfect.

They walked on in silence for a while and then Kurt said, 'I . . . I've never told anyone this but I received a letter from a neighbour to say my mother and sisters were taken to a concentration camp. I've no idea if they're still alive.'

'Oh, Sonny, I'm so sorry. What a terrible burden to carry. How can you bear it?'

'I used to think that if I threw everything I had into the effort to stop Hitler from carrying out any more atrocities, it would help ease my pain and somehow, I could win everything back . . . but now I really don't know. I've been completely focused on my job as a bomber pilot. And inside, I feel empty. It's as if I've lost everything and I'll never get it back. Leo says I ought to grab whatever's there and live for the moment. Perhaps he's right. Who knows what the future holds?'

'Kitty thinks like that too. For two people who think so alike, they spend a lot of time apart.'

'I know. I keep telling Leo to stop playing around with other girls who mean nothing to him and let Kitty know she's the one. But he seems incapable. Still, what would I know? I'm hardly an expert on romance. I'm the man who gave a girl a heart when it should have been a horseshoe or a rabbit's foot. I'm also the fool who walked away from you . . . ' He hesitated. 'I don't want to press you, Ellie, but it would mean so much to me if we could see more of each other . . . '

No! her inner voice said.

'Yes, I'd like that, Sonny.'

'Perhaps a walk in the woods tomorrow? I'm not sure when I need to be back at base but we should have a few hours together if we leave here at about oh nine hundred.'

'That would be lovely.'

When they reached Larkrise Farm, she said, 'D'you mind if I call you Kurt when we're alone? It's the name I first knew you by.'

'Of course.' He reached out and

stroked her cheek with his thumb. 'Like a new beginning?'

He turned to walk back down the path. 'See you tomorrow,' he said, his face alight with pleasure.

As Ellie let herself into the farmhouse, she held her hand to the cheek where Kurt had just stroked her, reliving the thrill of his touch.

She lay in bed, trying to quash her misgivings. He'd told her he'd stopped seeing her because he wasn't able to concentrate on flying when he was emotionally linked to her. He wouldn't risk his crew's safety and lives, so if he'd suggested they spend more time together, then he must only regard her as a friend. And that would be fine.

Who are you trying to fool? demanded her inner voice.

* * *

Kurt arrived just before nine o'clock the next morning, clutching a paper bag.

'Cake!' he said. 'I'm sorry, I couldn't get a picnic. I have to be back soon. There's an important mission planned for today.'

It was promising to be fine and dry, the late August sun already beating down as they walked. At the stile Kurt helped Ellie climb over, keeping hold of her hand as they wandered beneath the towering, leafy branches which filtered the light, making the world appear dappled green.

They sat by a stream and as they ate the cake, Kurt spoke about his childhood in Berlin and how different his life had been with Jack and Sylvia in Whitechapel. For the first time Ellie spoke about her childhood and how she'd escaped her mother's plans to find her a husband.

Ellie was disappointed when Kurt checked his watch and told her it was time he went.

'Perhaps we could do this again — as friends?' Ellie asked. To her dismay, Kurt seemed unsure.

'I don't know. I . . . I . . . suppose I was hoping we could become more than friends.'

'Oh, I see. I don't know, Kurt, I just don't know.'

'I wouldn't hurt you, Ellie! I know I behaved stupidly before but I wouldn't do that again.'

'But what about your crew? I thought you wanted to put them first.'

'I do and I will. But I see things differently now. I was talking to Tony, my rear gunner, and he said that far from distracting him, thoughts of his fiancée made him more determined to return alive. My main aim used to be to bomb and destroy the targets. Getting home was a bonus. But if I had someone to come home for, I'd be more determined than ever to get back . . . But don't tell me now. Perhaps you'll think about it.'

Ellie hesitated. 'Y . . . yes, all right.'

'Ellie? Would you wave me off tonight?'

'Y . . . yes. All right, I'll be there.'

He placed his hand over his chest and as she touched it lightly, they smiled at each other, knowing they were sharing thoughts.

* * *

Ellie was brushing her hair, ready to leave early for the airfield when there was a knock on the door. She assumed it was Jean or Maggie, who'd moved into the room opposite when Jess and Genevieve had left. They were quiet girls and she hadn't seen much of them since they'd been billeted at Larkrise Farm.

However, it was neither of the two new WAAFs. It was a rather angry-looking Mrs Ringwood.

'Is your friend here?' she asked, arms folded across her large bosom and her expression stern.

'No, I'm afraid not,' said Ellie politely, wondering what Kitty had done now to annoy Mrs Ringwood. She checked her watch. 'Her shift finished a little while ago, so I'm sure she'll be back very soon.'

Mrs Ringwood snorted with derision. 'Or out with yet another man.'

Ellie's mouth opened to protest but she could hardly deny that was a possibility. Kitty hadn't been very discreet lately and Ellie knew Mrs Ringwood's friends in the village liked to gossip.

'Well, when she gets back, I'll tell her you'd like to see her,' Ellie said, hoping her reasonable tones would calm Mrs Ringwood.

From downstairs, they heard the door opening and a chair scraping across the floor.

'Whoops!' It was Kitty.

Mrs Ringwood's brows knit together and she thundered down the wooden stairs, followed by Ellie. In the kitchen, Kitty was holding on to the back of the chair she'd obviously fallen against.

'Drunk? At this hour?' Mrs Ringwood was outraged. 'You're an absolute disgrace.'

Kitty had the good grace to appear ashamed. With exaggerated care, she straightened the chair and apologised but her words were slurred.

Ellie winced. This was something new. Kitty had always known when to stop because alcohol affected her very quickly, but recently, she'd been spending time with one of the new pilots and he liked a drink.

'I've had complaints,' Mrs Ringwood said, pushing Kitty's hands off the back of the chair and then crossing her arms over her chest.

'Complaints?' Kitty echoed.

'That's what I said! Complaints about you. So I expect you to pack your bags and go. All the WAAFs I've had staying here have been fine. But you! You're a disgrace to your uniform and I shall tell your commanding officer. You've got to the end of the month to sort out a new billet. That's generous. There's folk I know who'd put your things out on the doorstep and leave you to it.'

'But Mrs Ringwood!' Kitty said, appearing to sober up quickly. 'Please! Who's made complaints? Whatever they are, I'll change!'

'Your fellow WAAFs, that's who,' Mrs Ringwood said. 'All that drunkenness during the night, shouting and falling about! It's not fair on hardworking folk!'

'That's not right, Mrs Ringwood,' said Ellie, stepping forward to defend her friend. 'Kitty's not drunk at night, the noise is because — '

Kitty, realising Ellie was about to tell the farmer's wife about her nightmares and sleepwalking, stepped forward and cut in.

'I'll change, Mrs Ringwood, I promise.'

Ellie knew this was a promise Kitty would be unable to keep but Mrs Ringwood hadn't finished.

'Change! Huh! You're untidy, disruptive and as for the men! Don't get me started on that!'

'But I've never brought anyone back

here!' Kitty protested.

'I should think not!' Mrs Ringwood shrieked. She wagged her finger at Kitty. 'I've seen women of your sort before and they all come to a bad end. But I don't want your loose morals and bad behaviour rubbing off on any of the other WAAFs. So you can pack your bags and be on your way. You've got until the end of the month.'

She turned, stomped back to her sitting room and closed the door firmly behind her.

Ellie rushed to Kitty and put her arm around her. She might have behaved badly but Ellie knew that blasé façade hid a fragile girl who'd lost her way in life and craved affection.

Kitty wiped away tears with her handkerchief.

'You know who complained, don't you?' Kitty said between snivels.

Ellie didn't know for sure but the only people who'd have heard Kitty's cries at night were Jean and Maggie, the new girls.

Kitty marched up the stairs and knocked loudly on their bedroom door. It opened a crack and Jean peeped out. From her anxious expression, it was obvious she'd heard everything and knew exactly why Kitty was there.

'No hard feelings,' she said. 'It's just Maggie an' me can't sleep when you're making that racket at night. And Maggie says our reputation's under threat while we're under the same roof.'

'If you felt like that, you could've told me first,' Kitty said.

'Maggie said she didn't think you'd listen . . . '

Kitty turned away and Jean quickly closed her door. The awkward conversation was over.

Ellie followed Kitty into their bedroom.

'We've got until the end of the month,' she said gently, her arm around Kitty's shoulders.

'We? It's not you Mrs Ringwood wants to go, Ellie.'

'You don't think I'd let you go alone, do you?'

'Oh, Ellie, you're such a good friend. I don't deserve you. I don't know what I'd do without you. But no point you suffering because of me.'

'We're friends. We'll find something together.'

'You know what?' Kitty asked, standing up. 'That's a good idea. And I know what we're going to do. Come on!'

'Kitty! Where are you going?'

'Into the village. Come on! I know exactly what to do but I want you to see it first.'

'What? See what? Kitty, slow down!'

But Kitty had rushed down the stairs and was already outside.

Ellie put her shoes on and followed just as the clock on the kitchen mantelpiece chimed. She groaned. The Wellingtons would be lined up on the runway, ready for take-off and she hadn't been there to wave goodbye to Kurt as she'd promised. He would take off believing she hadn't wanted to see him.

As Ellie stepped out of the farmhouse, she heard the low rumble of the Wimpys trundling along the runway and the roar as they took off. Too late to do anything about that now. She ran after Kitty, with a heart as heavy as stone.

* * *

'Kitty! Wait!' Ellie ran down the path.

'Have you got any money?' Kitty asked when she'd caught up. 'I've only got two pennies. I'll need more than that.'

'Where are we going?' Ellie asked, anxious to know they weren't going to the Wild Boar.

'To the telephone box to telephone my father.'

'What for?'

'Because he's the answer to my problems. Well, in this instance, anyway.'

Ellie remembered the tall man with thick, grey hair who'd greeted Kitty at GC's funeral. He was an Air Marshal, so would obviously be able to influence any decisions made about Kitty — if he wanted to. And when Mrs Ringwood made her complaints to the WAAF section officer, Kitty was likely to be in trouble.

Ellie fished in her pocket and came out with a handful of change, which she held out.

'Is that enough?' she asked.

'Let's hope so,' Kitty said.

'Won't your father be angry?' Ellie asked. 'About you getting into trouble with the section officer.'

'Oh, I shan't tell him about that.'

'Well, what is it you're going to ask him for?'

'I'll show you. Look, just up there.'

'That?' Ellie asked incredulously, pointing to a rundown cottage surrounded by a neglected, overgrown garden ahead on the left.

'That's it.'

'Kitty, you're not making any sense.'

'When I was in the Wild Boar the other day, one of the villagers was talking about selling the cottage. His father died a few months ago. Charles thought he might buy it as an investment for when the war's over but his navigator talked him out of it, saying it needed too much work.'

'But surely you're not thinking of buying it?'

'No, I can't afford it. But my father can. And I'm certain he will.'

Ellie paused. 'He'll buy it for you just because you ask?'

'Well,' Kitty's voice took on a bitter tone, 'I may have to remind him who I am. But once he's remembered he's got a daughter, he'll buy it.'

'Kitty! That's very harsh!'

'Harsh, yes. But true.' Kitty sighed. 'Since my mother died ten years ago, he's had no time for me. It's like I don't exist. He put me in an expensive boarding school, sent generous amounts of money for birthdays and Christmas but the thing he's never given me is his time.'

'Oh, Kitty, I'm so sorry. That must've

been hard for you.'

'I get by,' Kitty said quietly.

They stood at the broken garden gate. *Lilac Cottage*, the sign declared although if there had once been lilacs in the garden, they were now buried under the weeds and brambles.

'I'm sure it'll look completely different when it's had a lick of paint,' Kitty said. 'And it's got two bedrooms, so we won't have to share . . . that is, unless you want to stay with Mrs Ringwood . . . I wouldn't charge you rent,' she added quickly.

'Oh, Kitty, that's very kind. And I wouldn't want to stay at Larkrise Farm without you.'

'So, you'll move in with me?'

'Well, aren't you forgetting something? It's not yours yet.'

'That's just a formality,' Kitty said.

'D'you know what it's like inside?' Ellie asked.

'Well, Charles and I peeped through the windows and went round to the back garden. It's tiny but I'm sure it's fine. I don't know what it's like upstairs, though. The owner told Charles it had two bedrooms, so that's how I know.'

'Who is this Charles you keep talking about?' Ellie asked with a sinking feeling. There was only one pilot called Charles that she knew of at the station and she was desperately hoping that it wasn't him. She'd seen his file, and knew that he lived away from the station with his wife. And not only that, but he'd been disciplined at his previous station for having indiscriminate affairs.

'Charles Donaldson. He's one of the pilots — '

'Oh, Kitty! Please tell me you're just friends.'

'Well . . . '

'Kitty, I'm really sorry to tell you this but he's already married.'

'Oh, darling! I know. Goodness, you looked so serious, I thought something dreadful had happened to him.'

'You *know?*'

'Well, of course. He's so honest, Ellie.

And charming. So much more grown-up than the others like Leo.'

'That's because he's twenty-eight — he's an old man compared to Leo and Sonny.'

'Well, I know they talk about him as if he's ancient but really, he's so mature. And so caring.'

'But he's *married*.'

'Just for the moment.'

'Kitty, please don't tell me he's said he's leaving his wife for you!'

'He is! He's just sorting out a few legal details and then we'll be together.'

Ellie sighed. There was no point getting into an argument with Kitty over Charles Donaldson. It was obvious she didn't want to hear anything against him. And fairly soon, his eye would rest on someone else. Hopefully very soon.

'This is the real thing, darling,' Kitty said.

'But what about Leo?'

'Leo?' Kitty considered for a few seconds. 'Well, I thought he was the one but it's obviously not meant to be. He can't keep his hands off other women and while he pays attention to them, I simply look elsewhere. It'll never work.'

Ellie waited outside the telephone box while Kitty spoke to her father. She wished Mrs Ringwood had chosen another time to tell Kitty she wanted her to leave. If she had, then Ellie would have made it to the airfield in time to say goodbye to Kurt. She decided she'd wake early, go the airfield and wait for the return of the Wellingtons. She'd missed saying goodbye but at least she'd be there to welcome him home.

Kitty replaced the receiver with a thumbs-up sign to Ellie.

'It should be mine before the end of the month, with any luck,' Kitty said with a triumphant smile as she came out of the box. 'He wasn't happy but I look at it this way, I've done him a service. At least it'll cost him so much, it'll salve his conscience and he won't have to feel guilty about ignoring me for quite a while.'

5

After the briefing, the crews of the Wellingtons dispersed to prepare for take-off in a few hours' time.

Kurt wasn't very hungry but he returned to the officers' mess with Leo for a meal.

'What are you looking at, Sonny?' Leo asked as Kurt peered through the window. 'Or should I say, who are you looking for?'

'Well, if you must know, Ellie said she'd come and say goodbye.'

Leo whistled. 'Ellie! Is it back on between you two, then?'

'It doesn't look like it.'

'It's early yet. She wouldn't be allowed into the Officers' Mess, so she's not going to stand around outside for ages.'

'Perhaps.' Although Ellie had said she'd come, she'd looked rather doubtful. Perhaps she'd changed her mind.

But still, Leo might be right — she might not yet have arrived.

They finished their meal and then after one last look outside, a disappointed Kurt followed Leo to the crew room to meet up with their respective crews who were putting on boots and flying gear, ready for their mission to the Ruhr.

Kurt looked out of the truck which would take them to their waiting aircraft near the runway. Ellie wasn't there. If she turned up at all, she would see him take off but he wouldn't be able to see her. And that had been the point of inviting her. He desperately wanted to see her.

A feeling of impending disaster gripped him and he looked about at his men, to try to judge their mood. Everyone seemed just as they normally did before a mission.

Everything is normal, he told himself and placed his hand against his chest. When the truck drew up at P for Pip, Kurt and his men climbed out and were met by their ground crew.

'All ready for you, sir,' the sergeant said to Kurt, saluting.

Climbing up into the nose of the aircraft after his crew, Kurt touched his locket again as he usually did and imagined Leo climbing aboard G for George, patting his Wimpy as he entered, allowing the ring he wore on his right hand, to come into contact with the fuselage before he put his glove on. And all along the line of bombers, pilots were performing whatever ritual they usually carried out to bring them luck that night.

After checking his crew, Kurt made his way back to the cockpit, sat down, put on his helmet and switched the intercom on. Then satisfied everyone was ready, he started the engines, checked his controls and signed the engine log which was passed to the sergeant outside. The steps were taken away and the hatch closed, then Kurt ordered the chocks to be removed. He steered the aircraft to the end of the runway, to join the queue of Wimpys about to take off.

The tail light of the aircraft in front disappeared into the darkening sky and Kurt gave the order, 'Stand by, crew, ready for take-off.'

He glanced back at the base, wondering if Ellie was there watching. He didn't think so. She'd hesitated when he'd asked her and he'd seen her brows draw together and the look of uncertainty in her eyes. In a few weeks, she'd changed from the easy-going, spontaneous girl he'd accompanied home that first time, to a serious, aloof woman.

How the war had changed them all!

At the sign of the green light, he pushed the throttles forward, propelling the machine along the runway, then up, into the night sky heading for the industrial Ruhr Valley.

As they approached their target, Kurt could see points of yellow light ahead in the darkness and knew the Pathfinders had made the job of the Wellington crews easier by marking out where they should drop their bombs.

The German searchlights played across the sky, illuminating the Wellingtons for the antiaircraft guns. Kurt wove through the beams and the flak, keeping an eye on the other aircraft to avoid a mid-air collision.

Once the bombs had been dropped, Kurt turned the plane away from the searchlight beams with relief, heading home.

'Captain to Wireless Operator. Send the message 'Mission completed',' he said into the intercom.

Kurt and his crew prepared for the journey home.

* * *

Ellie got up at first light, trying not to disturb Kitty, and walked to the station with Jean and Maggie who were both on duty in the ops room.

'Come and have a mug of tea,' Jean said to Ellie, 'there's time before the men are due back.'

Ellie was still drinking hers when Jean and Maggie started their new shift, taking over from the WAAFs who'd been on duty when the squadron left for the Ruhr.

'I've got a Darky Emergency Call!' Ellie heard one of the girls in the ops room call. 'The pilot's lost. He's not one of ours but he's nearly out of fuel, the aircraft's been hit, he's lost a wing tip and he thinks the undercarriage is jammed.'

Ellie finished her tea and went outside to watch and pray as the unknown fighter pilot in his Spitfire who'd put out the 'Darky Call' was guided in by the WAAFs inside the ops room. It loomed out of the growing mist, listing heavily to one side — with no undercarriage down, its prospects looked dire. The emergency vehicles were standing by ready to assist as soon as it landed — or crashed.

'So many men!' Ellie whispered to the night. 'So many lives hanging in the balance each and every mission.'

She found she was pressing her hand to her chest, hoping, hoping. For this pilot and of course, for Kurt and his crew who were due back shortly.

The Spitfire was going too fast. Even Ellie, with her limited experience of landing procedure, could tell that, and it was tilting even more than it had been in the air. As it neared the runway, the damaged wing caught on the ground, flipping the aircraft over and over. When it finally came to rest, it was upside down and flames had started to appear, licking the fuselage.

Sirens blared, the fire roared, men shouted as the emergency vehicles raced to the burning Spitfire and men scurried into and out of the clouds of black smoke. Further explosions followed, sending them running for cover.

Ellie saw the wing commander on the watch tower with his binoculars trained on the fire, then as a WAAF spoke to him, he turned and peered up into the sky, pointing.

'What's happening?' Ellie asked one of the ground crew who'd just come on duty.

'Gotta go,' he gasped. 'Gotta make sure the runway's clear. One of ours is coming in.' He ran off, putting his jacket on as he went.

Ellie ran back inside the ops block.

With calm efficiency, the plotters moved their blocks around the table and one by one, the Wellingtons landed and taxied back to their hangars.

Ellie strained her ears, listening intently for some mention of P for Pip returning. It seemed that all but four aircraft had returned and only P for Pip, G for George, L for London and Q for Queen were still unaccounted for.

'L for London's on its way. It's nearly out of fuel but the squadron leader thinks with the wind speed and direction, it might just glide in. Everyone's on standby . . . ' Ellie heard someone say. But still no news on the other three aircraft.

Jean came out of the ops room to

make mugs of tea and caught sight of Ellie.

'I didn't know you were still here, Ellie, are you all right?'

'I'm waiting to find out about a friend . . . He's the pilot of P for Pip . . . '

Jean sighed and shook her head. 'We're pretty certain Q for Queen went down in the Channel but as for P for Pip and G for George, we just don't know. I'm so sorry, Ellie. But your friend could still come in. Or more likely, he's issued a Darky Call which some other station's picked up and they've guided our men in. They're probably sitting in the mess now, drinking tea.'

She patted Ellie's shoulder.

Ellie smiled. She knew Jean was trying to cheer her up but there was so much that could've gone wrong.

'Why don't you go home?' Jean said. 'You look exhausted.'

'No, I want to stay until . . . well, until . . . '

Jean nodded sadly.

'OK, well we should have some news soon.'

Ellie wandered back outside and looked along the runway.

Lights could be seen emerging from the mist, and for a second, hope rose in her. She ran back into the ops block but to her disappointment, the aircraft that was about to land, was L for London. It had been hit by flak, damaging the fuel tank and the undercarriage which wouldn't lower.

Ellie went back outside to watch the emergency vehicles get into position on the runway and remembered how the Spitfire pilot had tried to land without wheels.

The huge Wellington came in, approaching the runway slowly — almost like a ghost. Then, it hit the ground, bounced, rose, landed again and gradually slid to a stop. She saw the men emerge, and the captain, waiting for all his crew to leave before he too, jumped down to the ground.

Members of the ground crew congratulated them and once the air crew walked away, they swarmed over the fuselage, checking the damage.

Ellie exhaled. She'd not dared breathe until L for London was down safely. She was so pleased for the captain and crew. But still P for Pip, G for George and Q for Queen had not come home.

* * *

Ahead, Kurt could see the Belgian coast and beyond that, the dark waters of the Channel. To the starboard and slightly below him, was G for George and beyond that, almost out of sight, was Q for Queen. Not much further to go and then the coast of England would be visible.

From out of the cloud cover above them all, a formation of Messerschmitts swooped, and as Kurt swung the aircraft to the left, he felt the stammer of guns from the rear gun turret as Tony

Williams fired at the enemy craft.

Two of the Messerschmitts peeled off to pursue Leo and Mike Howley, the pilot of Q for Queen, leaving the other planes to follow Kurt. Tony's aim was good and one of the enemy aircraft exploded in a brilliant yellow flash, then spiralled towards the water below. But another Messerschmitt was more adept at dodging Tony's shots and it continued the chase, its bright tracer bullets slicing through the night sky and striking P for Pip on the starboard wing with sharp cracks.

As the fighter turned, bullets whipped past Kurt's head, leaving neat holes in the Perspex windscreen. He realised one of them had grazed his shoulder but there was no time to check. He could still use his arm, so it couldn't be too bad.

The vibrations coming from the engine and its irregular rhythm told Kurt it had been damaged by the German bullets. Immediately Pat Harkness, the flight engineer, reported that the wing had also been badly damaged with gaping holes in the fabric — but more importantly, there was a fuel leak from the tanks.

Kurt held his hand over his chest, pressing the locket into his skin.

The damage was serious and the Messerschmitt was still on their tail.

Far to his right, an explosion caught his eye. It was a Wimpy — either Leo or Mike, he couldn't be sure — hanging for a second in the night sky like a bright flower, then plummeting into the sea. The other plane had also been hit and flames shot out of one wing as it spiralled down, nose first, into the water. The two Messerschmitts which had gone after Leo and Mike soared upwards and away. Their work was done.

But there was no time for Kurt to think about the fate of his two fellow pilots and their crews because the remaining Messerschmitts were heading straight for him. Tony rattled off more rounds but after another volley of cannon fire, the Germans ascended into the clouds and out of sight and the pilot who'd shelled P for Pip, followed.

Perhaps, thought Kurt, *they think they've damaged us too badly to get back to England. They may be correct.*

'Captain! Tony's been hit!' shouted Ralph Baker, the navigator. 'Bullets to the leg. I'm applying a tourniquet now.'

Oh God! Not Tony! Kurt had met the gunner's fiancée once and knew that shortly, they should be enjoying their wedding.

He gripped the controls tighter and winced at the pain in his arm. He must get the men back. He must . . .

'Everyone else all right?' he asked.

'There's a lot of damage back here and the wireless isn't operational,' said the wireless operator, Larry Butcher. 'I can't transmit or receive. So we're on our own.'

Kurt diverted the fuel, conserving it in the hope they'd reach land. There was no possibility of making it to Holsmere or even to an airfield, but they might just find a farmer's field somewhere which would offer them enough space to land on — or even to bail out over.

Kurt looked down at the dark water below and forced the image from his mind of Leo, Mike and their crews plunging into its depths.

Then, of course, there was the possibility they'd encounter more German fighter planes and now, with the rear gunner out of action . . .

However, they'd flown into a bank of thick mist which would give them cover while they tried to reach England. According to Ralph, the coast should have been in sight but the mist was thickening by the second.

Then just as Kurt had begun to think they were lost, the white cliffs loomed ahead — appearing ethereal in the mist. He knew with relief that they'd make it to land, even if they wouldn't be able to fly much further.

He must keep his nerve.

Now, the green fields of Kent lay

below and Kurt turned the aircraft to avoid several small villages.

'Captain to crew: Get ready to bail out!' Kurt said into his intercom.

He pulled the nose of the Wimpy up a little to give them a bit more height, so that with luck there would be enough distance between the men and the ground for their parachutes to open safely.

'Captain! Look!' Ralph said, pointing. 'Is that a runway?'

Ahead of them, about three miles away, a narrow strip lay.

'I believe it's RAF Cranes Heath,' Ralph said. 'But Larry can't warn them we're coming in.'

'We'll just have to hope the Observation Corps are taking note, then,' Kurt said. 'And keep our fingers crossed nothing else is landing at the same time.'

Kurt held his breath, as they glided closer and closer to the runway.

With his senses heightened, he took in the entire scene below — officers on the watch tower, pointing and running about, men on the ground emerging from hangars.

As he readied himself to land, he could even see pilots still in their flying suits, walking back to their mess, just as he would have done, had he made it back to Holsmere.

At the sound of his labouring engine with the staccato beat, the pilots turned and ran back towards the runway to assist.

Kurt's attention was entirely on his instruments and the rapidly approaching runway. At least everyone on the station knew they were coming in and could alert any other planes which might be about to land.

The approach was too fast and wildly out of control after the bullets' damage to the engine, the propeller and the wing, but Kurt hung on, swinging the aircraft away from the buildings. As it tipped over to one side, one wing dug deeply into the ground with a shower of sparks and for a second, it appeared the machine would cartwheel along the runway. But it fell over sideways and spun along, still at great speed, finally righting itself and coming to a shuddering halt.

The impact showered Kurt with shattered Perspex and threw him sideways with such force, he felt a sharp twinge in the arm he'd previously broken. Painfully, he disentangled himself and checked the crew.

So far, against all odds, everyone was alive, including Tony. He helped each one out of P for Pip before he, too, left.

Everywhere smelled of fuel and it would only take one small spark to start an inferno. The ambulance men met them on the runway and took Tony away on a stretcher.

As Kurt raced after his men across the runway away from the aircraft, he held his right arm to his chest to try to stop the pain as he ran, and briefly touched his chest to give thanks for their lucky escape.

The crew of P for Pip had somehow survived — although Tony was badly injured. The crews of G for George and Q for Queen had not been so lucky.

* * *

Kurt and his crew were taken to hospital where it was found he'd broken his arm in several places and a bullet had grazed his shoulder. Tony was taken away for an operation.

The other men were treated and kept in for observation before being sent back to Holsmere.

'Don't look so downhearted,' the sister said to Kurt. 'You're lucky to be alive, from what I've heard. Your rear gunner is stable and you'll be able to follow your men home in due course.

'And you're not alone here. We've just had a few more men admitted from your neck of the woods. When you're feeling up to it, they're in Patience Ward, just along the corridor. I want none of your RAF pilot high jinks though, please. The men are not in a good way.'

She tucked a blanket around his legs, plumped his pillows and walked briskly to the next bed.

From your neck of the woods. He wasn't sure what she meant. Perhaps aircrew from RAF Debden or North Weald. They were fairly near Holsmere. Or perhaps she simply meant from somewhere in Essex.

It was time he stretched his legs. It would be good to have some other chaps to talk to. The men in the beds on either side of him had both suffered burns and their heads were swathed in bandages, making it hard for them to talk.

'Yes?' the sister of Patience Ward said, holding her hand up to stop Kurt. 'Can I help you?'

'I was told there were some other airmen from Essex in here.'

'Two,' she said, pointing to the far corner. 'One is currently with the doctor. The other is in bed six. Don't tire him.'

Kurt wandered to the end of the

ward, wishing he hadn't come. Would they be burned like the men in his ward? If so, they probably wouldn't want to chat.

The fair-haired patient in bed six was asleep, his face turned to the pillow. Kurt stooped to read the name written on the notes at the end of the bed.

Daniel Vincent. It couldn't be!

'Leo?' Kurt said in disbelief, gripping the foot of the bed as his knees nearly gave way.

The patient woke as the contact made his bed tremble, and he looked up with bleary eyes.

'Sonny?' His voice shook with emotion.

* * *

'We went down into the drink,' Leo said. 'Air Sea Rescue found us . . . but in the end only Lofty and I made it,' he added, looking down.

Kurt told him about his landing at RAF Cranes Heath and for the first time since he'd found him, Leo smiled when he learned all of the crew had survived and that Tony would be fine.

'Mike in Q for Queen didn't make it,' Leo said. 'I saw them explode. They didn't stand a chance.'

Leo spoke as he always had — glossing over the tragedies. It was the airmen's coping mechanism. But Kurt detected a change in Leo. The bravado was no longer enough to hide the pain.

During the next few weeks while their injuries healed, Leo and Kurt spent a lot of time together, discussing the future.

'I keep thinking of Kitty,' Leo said. 'I've written but she hasn't replied. I'm not surprised, though. I didn't really treat her well.'

'She may not have had time to write,' Kurt said. 'You know how Hitler's ramped up the attacks. I've heard Holsmere's come under attack a few times since we left. Kitty's probably too busy.'

They both knew it would only take

moments to scribble a few words and put them in the post but neither said it. Kurt too, had been waiting for some word from Ellie. But none came.

A nurse had offered to write for him while his arm healed but he didn't want to speak his words out loud — not to anyone else. And anyway, Ellie had obviously made up her mind she didn't want him in her life.

6

Kurt had been correct. Life at Holsmere had been hectic while he and Leo had been in hospital recovering.

On the twentieth of August, Winston Churchill gave a stirring speech in the House of Commons.

'Never in the history of mankind has so much been owed by so many to so few,' he told the members of the House, paying tribute the courageous, determined airmen who'd so far managed to prevent Germany from gaining air supremacy over Britain.

But Hitler and the commander-in-chief of The Luftwaffe, Hermann Göring, had not given up. German attacks on RAF bases increased and after several Luftwaffe aircraft drifted off course and accidentally bombed London homes, killing civilians, Churchill ordered the RAF to attack Berlin in retaliation.

Hitler was incensed and commanded bombing raids to be carried out on London and other major British cities. The first night of intense aerial bombardment on London was the seventh of September, beginning what people were soon calling The London Blitz.

Eight days later, the heaviest fighting took place in what became known as the Battle of Britain Day, with Germany losing fifty-six aircraft. After the fifteenth of September, daytime attacks on airfields decreased, although the Blitz continued, causing devastation in several British cities, including London.

Group Captain Jennings assembled everyone on RAF Holsmere and congratulated them on their efforts so far, warning that the war was far from over. At the dance which followed his speech, Ellie realised Kitty and Charles Donaldson had slipped away.

Since Kitty had moved into Lilac Cottage, she'd been seeing a lot of Charles although they'd always been discreet. Charles parked his car along the lane and walked to the cottage but still, Ellie was sure it was only a matter of time before Charles was caught — or he lost interest in Kitty and went back to his wife.

Kitty would hear nothing against him and was convinced he would one day be with her.

Ellie reflected how sad it was that Kitty was searching for the love she felt her father had denied her in the arms of so many different men, only to find one who would never be hers.

She'd had enough of the dance and slipped out of the NAAFI to begin the walk back to Lilac Cottage. It was further away from the base than Larkrise Farm but hopefully, by the time she got home, Charles would be gone.

Several men had asked her to dance and out of politeness she'd agreed, but there was no point giving them the impression she was interested. She'd let her guard down when she and Kurt had gone for a walk in the woods — and look where that had led.

The news of his crash landing at RAF Cranes Heath had not arrived at Holsmere until several hours later, during which time, she'd believed Kurt and his crew had died. It had been agony.

She'd started writing several times but had never finished a letter. What was there to say? And anyway, he hadn't written to her. Perhaps he was still angry she hadn't seen him off.

He and Leo had been in hospital for so long, she wondered if they'd ever be coming back. Perhaps they would become flying instructors, training new pilots, in which case, she'd probably never see Kurt again.

She came across Charles half way between his car and Lilac Cottage.

'You left the dance early, Ellie,' he said. 'Fancy a spin in the car?'

'No thank you. Where's Kitty?'

'Got a headache,' he said, jerking his head towards the cottage. 'But the night's young. Come on, we could drive down to the river.'

'I said no. Thank you,' she said, walking past. He was contemptible. How could Kitty not see it?

'Oh well, your loss. I'll be at the Wild Boar if you change your mind.'

Ellie walked on without replying.

* * *

A few days later, there was a knock at the door. Kitty was expecting Charles — but not for another half an hour. How like the arrogant pilot to come when it suited him.

Kitty was still in her bedroom getting ready and she called downstairs, 'If that's Charles, please can you let him in and tell him I won't be a moment, darling.'

Ellie was tempted to go into the back garden and pretend she hadn't heard but when there was another knock, she relented.

Charles thrust a bouquet into her

hands and with a leer, leaned forward to kiss her. She took the flowers and pulled her face back to avoid his lips. He laughed and entered uninvited.

'So,' he said, slapping Ellie on the bottom. 'Pleased to see me?'

'Not at all,' she said, filling a vase and putting the flowers in without bothering to arrange them. 'You're early. Kitty's still getting ready.'

'Kitty won't mind,' he said and before she could stop him, he took the stairs two at a time.

Ellie went to the front door poked her head out to check Charles hadn't left his car outside as he had the last time he'd visited. She peered up and down the lane but thankfully, if he'd brought his car, he'd parked it out of sight.

She mused that it might be a good thing if he were discovered — but it would also mean Kitty got into trouble. Surely the affair couldn't last much longer?

Across the lane, behind the hedge,

Leo peeped through the tangle of branches at Lilac Cottage. He and Sonny had just returned to Holsmere and they'd decided to have a few pints at the Wild Boar to celebrate being back on duty. But more importantly to Leo, they were also going to drop by Kitty's new cottage and say hello.

He hadn't been able to get Kitty out of his mind. Hours bobbing around in the cold, choppy Channel, wondering if anyone had heard the desperate Mayday call the wireless operator had managed to send before they dropped out of the sky, had given him time to reflect. He wanted to apologise . . . and he desperately wanted another chance.

Everyone had said he and Kitty belonged together. It had only been his stupidity which had prevented him seeing it. And who knew, if he got back with Kitty, Sonny and Ellie might give it another go? That would be perfect. Although he hadn't mentioned that to Sonny because he seemed very down whenever Ellie was mentioned.

As he got into Sonny's car, one of the new pilots ran up to ask them for a lift into the village.

'Off to see your girl?' Leo asked, nodding at the bouquet the pilot held.

He agreed but when Leo asked if she was one of the WAAFs, all the pilot would say, was that it was all 'a bit hush-hush'.

Well, it was none of Leo's business. But when the pilot, who'd introduced himself as Charles Donaldson, asked to be let out at the crossroads, Leo began to wonder if his destination wasn't Lilac Cottage.

But if so, was he going to see Kitty or Ellie?

Of course, it could be somebody completely different. So many things had changed since he'd last been at Holsmere. Perhaps Kitty had other WAAFs staying with her at Lilac Cottage. Or perhaps someone was billeted at one of the other cottages further down the lane.

'I won't be a minute, Sonny, old

chap,' Leo said, scrambling out and squeezing through the hedge into the field, ignoring his friend's protests.

He reached the cottage in time to see Charles knock, present his flowers and lean forward to kiss the girl who'd opened the door.

It was Ellie!

Leo was thrilled and disappointed. Thrilled that Kitty wasn't involved with the insufferable pilot but disappointed for Sonny. Not that he'd expressed any interest in Ellie but Leo knew better.

Seconds later, Ellie opened the door and looked right and left. If Leo had been in any doubt she'd opened the door to Charles, he had none now.

* * *

'I'm sorry, Sonny,' Leo said when he got back to the car and explained what he'd seen.

Kurt was silent as he accelerated away.

'Only to be expected, I suppose,' he

said finally. 'We've been away a while. So much has changed. Does it seem like that to you?'

'Yes,' replied Leo. 'But even so, I'm sorry.'

At the Wild Boar, Leo and Kurt met up with many of the ground crew they'd known before and spent longer in the bar than they'd planned, buying pints for the men who worked so tirelessly on their aircraft.

Kurt felt a hand on his shoulder and looked around to see Charles Donaldson.

'Can I have a word, old man?' Charles asked.

It took all Kurt's self-control not to shake his hand off and tell him he didn't want a word with him. But what would that achieve? It certainly wouldn't get Ellie back.

Charles steered him away from the others.

'Are you planning to go to the dance in town on Saturday, old man? Only if you are, I wondered if you'd do me a great favour. I'll be going, but not until a bit later, so I won't be able to give my girl a lift there. I wondered if you'd oblige?'

Kurt stared at him, unable to believe what the man was asking. But then, he reminded himself, Charles would have had no idea he knew Ellie — much less that they had once been close.

Charles assumed Kurt's silence signalled that he was agreeing and awaiting further instructions.

'So, if you pick her up at about seven at Lilac Cottage. It's a bit further down that lane you dropped me off at — '

'I know where Lilac Cottage is,' Kurt snapped.

'Splendid. Well, the good news is that if you're not already taken, my girl's best friend is going to the dance too. I could put in a word for you?'

Kurt wanted to punch him on the nose, but his hand hadn't healed properly after his arm had been smashed in the crash. Then he had an idea.

'Leave it to me,' he said and brushing

off Charles' hand from his shoulder, he went back to his friends at the bar.

'What did he want?' Leo asked.

'I'll tell you later. But don't make any arrangements for Saturday evening.'

'I didn't know you knew Donaldson,' Tim Graham, one of the flight mechanics said, scowling at Charles' back.

'I don't,' said Kurt, 'not really.'

'Good,' said Tim, ''e's trouble. There's going to be a tremendous flap about 'im very soon.'

'One of the mechanics knew Donaldson at another airfield. 'E's married but 'e can't keep 'is 'ands off the women. But worse than that. It looks like 'e's falsified records. 'E makes mistakes and covers 'em up by blaming anyone around 'im. 'Is crew don't want to fly with 'im any more. Several of 'is ground crew 'ave got in trouble because of his mistakes and now, 'e's been reported. Yup, there's going to be a right old flap, if you ask me.'

* * *

Kurt decided to go to the dance at the last minute. He hadn't been planning to go once he'd persuaded Leo to pick Kitty and Ellie up in his car. It was the perfect opportunity for Leo to make amends to Kitty. Of course, it was agonising to think of Leo taking Ellie to the dance so she could meet Charles. But Ellie had made her decision to be with him, and Kurt must respect that.

Respect. He was finding it hard to respect a girl who was seeing a married man. But it was possible she didn't know.

Then, on Friday, Kurt was walking across the parade ground when he saw Charles with his kit bag, accompanied by the wing commander, walking towards his car. As the pilot drove away, the senior officer stood shaking his head sadly.

Kurt walked in his direction and saluted.

'Ah, Flight Lieutenant Rayment. It's a sad day. I need to be able to trust my men.' He turned on his heel and went back to the Officers' Mess.

Tim Graham, the mechanic, was more voluble.

'Good riddance to bad rubbish. Donaldson won't be back. Cuppa?' he asked Kurt, and told him all about the pilot's misdemeanours.

Kurt didn't tell Leo about Charles' departure. His friend was looking forward to being with Kitty so much, it didn't seem worth bothering him but he suddenly realised that Ellie would be expecting Charles to meet her at the dance. When she found out he'd left, she'd obviously be upset. But if he was there, he could offer her a lift home. She'd be sad, of course, but he'd simply be there in case she needed a friend.

* * *

Ellie hadn't wanted to go to the dance but she knew Charles had arranged for someone to take Kitty and that he was going to meet her later. She wanted to be there for her friend while she waited.

As soon as Charles turned up, she'd hitch a lift home.

Charles had said he'd arranged a date for her, but she didn't want to be with anyone — least of all a friend of Charles.

She'd been amazed to see Leo pull up outside Lilac Cottage and come up the path to collect them. But it was perfect! While Kitty waited for Charles, perhaps she could rekindle things with Leo. She decided she wouldn't go and then, the two would be alone together — at least until Charles turned up.

But Leo insisted she go and when Kitty learned she'd decided to stay home, she pleaded with her to join them.

The hall was packed and Ellie soon lost sight of Kitty and Leo who spent the first dances together. She craned her neck and glanced at the door anxiously, dreading Charles arriving and steering Kitty away from Leo.

'He won't be coming, I'm afraid, Ellie.'

She looked up and to her surprise, saw Kurt, his expression gentle and sympathetic.

'No need to pretend. I know all about Charles Donaldson.'

Ellie sighed. What must he think of Kitty?

'How d'you know he's not coming?'

'I saw him leave the base yesterday. He won't be back. I'm not sorry. But I imagine you'll miss him,' he said.

'Miss him? I couldn't wait to see the back of him! And thankfully, it doesn't look like Kitty's going to be too upset either,' she said pointing at Leo and Kitty who were waltzing past, staring into each other's eyes.

Kurt stepped back.

'Why would Kitty miss him?'

Ellie frowned. 'You said you knew all about it.'

'Well, I knew you and Charles were together, but Kitty . . . ?'

'Charles and me?' Ellie stood up. 'I couldn't stand the man! Excuse me!' She pushed past Kurt.

He caught her arm. 'Please, Ellie, I didn't mean to upset you. I think Leo might have got his facts wrong. Can I buy you a drink? Perhaps you'd tell me what's been going on . . . that's if you want to . . . It's none of my business, of course.'

She allowed herself to be led to a corner of the hall and Kurt explained about Leo watching Charles through the hedge at Lilac Cottage and how he'd seen him give Ellie flowers and kiss her.

'Tried to kiss me,' she said, wrinkling her nose in disgust, 'I actually dodged him. But yes, I suppose I can see why Leo might have got the wrong impression.'

'So, I'm forgiven?'

'Yes, of course. And I'm so grateful you've got Leo and Kitty together again.'

'Just call me Cupid!' he said with a smile.

Ellie laughed.

'Is there anyone you've got your eye

on?' he asked, 'I've still got a few arrows left.'

'Well, there was one man . . . ' she said, smiling sadly, 'but I think I upset him some time ago. You see, I promised to do something for him . . . but I wasn't able to.'

'Perhaps if you explained?' he said. 'I'm sure he might understand.'

'I'm so sorry, Kurt. I wanted to come to see you off that night before you crashed. It was just that — '

'You don't need to explain, Ellie. It's enough to know you meant to come. That means the world to me. I took off thinking you'd made a decision not to include me in your life.'

'I was there the next morning to see you land. But . . . you didn't come. I was frantic . . . and then once I knew you were safe, I thought it was for the best that I didn't contact you.'

'And do you still think it's for the best?'

'I don't know. I thought I could protect myself from all the pain that love seems to bring. But the truth is, I haven't been able to get you off my mind. I thought you wouldn't want to know me after I let you down.'

'I've thought about little else but you, Ellie.'

The band began a slow number and Kurt led her to the dance floor, then took her in his arms.

How right it felt to be close to him, holding him tightly. Ellie looked up and saw he'd been watching her, his dark eyes full of apprehension as if he knew she was struggling with her instincts to keep him at bay.

But the longer he held her close, the more she knew she couldn't bear to be parted from him.

Closing herself off from love hadn't enriched her life and it hadn't made her happy. Surely taking a chance and letting the fire of love ignite — even for a brief time, was better than feeling frozen and numb?

After the last waltz, Kurt drove Ellie back to Lilac Cottage.

'I'm free tomorrow if you'd like to go to the woods,' he said as he walked her to the door.

'Yes, I'd love that.' A few days before, she'd gone through the woods on her own but it was as if the world had turned grey. Sharing it with him would bring the colours to life.

'I can't tell you how happy I am tonight.' He put his arms around her waist, pulling her close.

'Me too.' She wrapped her arms around his neck and he bent towards her, gently kissing her.

'Until tomorrow,' he whispered but they still clung to each other, unwilling to let go.

He kissed her again, with more urgency and she pulled him closer, relishing the warmth of his body pressed closely to hers.

The sound of a car drawing up and Kitty's laugh brought them back to reality. Kurt kissed her forehead and with a smile, turned and walked down the path, calling over his shoulder,

'Until tomorrow.'

'Oh, hello,' said Kitty as she passed Kurt at the gate, 'I hope Leo and I didn't disturb you!'

* * *

If anything, the rich autumnal hues were brighter and more vibrant than Ellie had expected. It wasn't the trees, she knew. It was simply that Kurt was there with her.

She'd hardly slept all night, reliving the feeling of being enfolded in his arms as they danced and then later when he'd kissed her. She longed for morning, for Kurt to come, to hold his hand, to feel his lips again on hers.

How foolish she'd been to cut herself off from the possibility of love. They'd wasted so much time. And who knew how much time was left? The expected lifespan of a pilot was very short and so far, Kurt had survived for months. How much longer would his luck last? And then what would she do?

It suddenly came to her. If anything happened to Kurt, she would remember all these precious moments and hold them in her heart. She had no control over what happened to him; all she could do was to love him while he was there and enjoy every second.

By forbidding herself the pleasure of knowing him and loving him, she would end up with no memories at all — just an aching emptiness.

They went down to the river and watched the falling leaves tumble into the water, to be swept away, twirling in the current.

'When are you next free?' Kurt murmured, his mouth against her hair.

'Not until Monday. And you?'

'The same. Shall we go to London?'

Ellie watched the leaves spinning in the breeze as they fell. Kurt would be flying tomorrow. Suppose he didn't come back?

'If you don't want to go to London, we could go to Chelmsford,' he said tilting her chin up with his finger and looking deeply into her eyes. 'I don't care where we are, so long as we're together.'

He reached inside his shirt and hooking his finger under the chain, he lifted the heart-shaped locket out. Then, fumbling with the ring-bolt, he took it off.

'Here. I want you to have this.'

'No!' Ellie drew back. 'Put it on, Kurt! You need that for luck! I can't bear the thought of you being in danger. I don't know what I'd do if . . . '

'I'll be fine, Ellie,' he said with a smile, taking her hand and placing the necklace in her palm, 'trust me. Flying a desk is really quite safe.'

'What d'you mean?'

'I'm grounded. I won't be flying for some time.' He held out his right hand and flexed the fingers. 'Nerve damage,' he said. 'After I smashed it up. I don't have much strength in that hand, so I won't be able to fly until — or if — I regain full strength. So, in the meantime, I've got a desk job.'

'Oh, Kurt, I'm so sorry. I know it was important to you to be a pilot.'

'Not any more, Ellie. For so long, I wanted to avenge my family.' He sighed. 'But I've no idea where they are, nor if they're still alive. When the war's over, I'll go back to Germany and look for them. But there are more ways of winning the war than flying.'

Ellie threw her arms around his neck and kissed him.

'So, you'll keep the necklace?' he asked. 'I'd really like you to. It's probably the closest you'll ever get to meeting my family.'

Ellie held the locket up by the chain and watched it spin in the breeze. Taking it from her, Kurt fastened it around her neck, slipping it inside her shirt. She shivered as the cold locket slithered down her chest but she knew her body heat would soon warm it up.

He stooped to kiss the back of her hand as she placed it over the locket.

'I'm so pleased you accepted it,' he said, 'because that necklace is the most precious thing I own and I want you to have it because you're the most precious thing in my life. I know we haven't known each other long, Ellie, but everything's more intense with the war on. In peacetime, we might've taken things more slowly. But if we delay now, we may never get another chance. I love you and however much time I have left, I want to spend it with you.'

She put her arms around his neck. 'And I want to spend it with you, Kurt.'

A warm glow spread through her and she knew that her heart of ice had completely thawed.

Other titles in the
Linford Romance Library:

THE CHRISTMAS VISITOR

Jill Barry

Rich man's daughter Eleanor is horrified when her father invites disgraced nobleman Rupert to join the family Christmas house party. But when the pair meet by accident, she finds him attractive, then is dismayed to learn his identity. Rupert and his valet fit in well, while gentle scheming by the indispensable Mr Steadman enhances Eleanor and Rupert's dawning relationship. Upstairs and downstairs, romance blossoms — but can both his lordship and his valet make amends for their past mistakes?